No Cafés in Narnia
A Tarragon Island Novel

by Nikki Tate

Sono Nis Press

VICTORIA, BRITISH COLUMBIA

Canadian Cataloguing in Publication Data

Tate, Nikki, 1962-
  No cafés in Narnia

  ISBN 1-55039-107-0
  I. Title.
PS8589.A8735N62 2000   jC813'.54   C00-910806-8
PZ7.T2113No 2000

Sono Nis Press gratefully acknowledges the support of the
Canada Council for the Arts and the Province of British
Columbia, through the British Columbia Arts Council.

All quotations are from the following sources:
The Writer's Quotation Book: A Literary Companion,
edited by James Charlton, Penguin Books, 1986.
Bartlett's Familiar Quotations, Sixteenth Edition,
General Editor Justin Keplan, Little, Brown & Company, 1992.

Cover design by Jim Brennan

Published by
SONO NIS PRESS
PO Box 5550, Stn. B
Victoria, BC V8R 6S4
tel: (250) 598-7807
sono.nis@islandnet.com
http://www.islandnet.com/sononis/

Distributed in the U.S. by
Orca Book Publishers
Box 468
Custer, WA 98240-0468
1-800-210-5277

PRINTED AND BOUND IN CANADA BY FRIESEN'S PRINTING

For Mel and Sam,
with thanks.

Chapter One

Collected Quote #107
A writer is like a bag lady going through life with a sack and a pointed stick collecting stuff.—Tony Hillerman

Sometimes, when I'm nervous, I stare. It's like my eyes freeze open and I have to pay attention to every detail around me. I start noticing crazy things like the way the nostril hairs curl out of the guy's nose at the gas station. That happened when I pumped gas for my mother for the first time ever and I forgot the gas cap on the roof of the car. I heard this yelling just when I was getting in the car and I thought it was a robbery or something. So I jumped in and slammed the door and screamed at my mom, "Drive! Go!" Before we could get away there was this banging on the window and it was him! Nostril guy—waving the gas cap at me.

His nose hairs didn't come straight out of his nostrils like you might expect—they were long enough that they first curled clockwise and then twisted counterclockwise and though they were silver-tipped at the ends, at the base where they disappeared up into his nose those hairs were pitch black.

Noticing things when I'm nervous is just the start! Even stranger is how, inside my head, I start talking to myself like I'm telling a story about a girl just like me and I have to get all my observations exactly right. Writer Girl—that's what I call her—and right at this very moment she is making a lot of noise in my head.

I'm attending my first ever meeting of the TWYG (that's pronounced *twig*, like a small tree branch, but it stands for Tarragon Writing Youth Group). When I read the notice in the paper, it sounded like the perfect group for me. But now that I'm here at the Tarragon Island Community Centre, I am scared out of my wits. So, inside my head, this is what it sounds like.

Writer Girl, plump and attractive with dark, wavy hair, has been half swallowed by the Community Centre's bulgy, brown couch. She desperately wants to scratch her legs because the brown material is prickly but she's afraid that if she starts scratching, the others will think she has fleas. Whenever she moves even the teeniest bit, the cushions make a soft crackly noise like they are so old they're stuffed with straw. She has sunk so far into the couch her knees are higher than the rest of her.

This awkward position of mine on the couch is part of the reason I feel so out of place here in the writing group. The others all look so relaxed and know each other and they sprawl over the furniture like they've lived there forever. They've been meeting once a week for more than a year, ever since the Community Centre started a Youth for the Future campaign.

Writer Girl struggles valiantly to balance her notebook on her lap. She wants to write the most brilliant story she has ever dreamed up so the others in the group will be very impressed, but she's so busy staring at the squiggle designs on the bottom of Eric's running shoes, which are sticking out from under the coffee table attached to his skinny pair of legs, that she can't seem to get started.

It's true. I'm trying to pay attention and do every-thing right—the way the others in the writing group seem to be doing so easily, but the exercise is hard and confusing and I just can't seem to get going.

"Balloons."

Wynd, the girl trapped in the couch beside me, blurts out the word and four pens in the room fly across pages in tattered notebooks. Mine doesn't fly anywhere. It's sort of sluggish in my hand, like an alien object I don't quite know how to use. It reminds me of how it feels when I try to write with my left hand: awkward.

Writer Girl, superhero of her generation, battles fever-ishly against the forces of writer's block and acute embarrassment. She is determined to let her ideas flow onto the page, to create a masterpiece even if it kills her. She ignores the heavy slab of hair that slides across her cheek as she bends forward over her notebook, pen tip poised above the page.

Balloons? What the heck kind of story could possibly include the word *balloons*? The whole point of this exercise is we're not supposed to know where the story will wind up since we have no way of knowing who is going to blab out the next word. I can't work like this. I need to have a plan, to know where I'm going.

"Pig," Eric says from where he's stretched out on his belly on the floor.

Balloons? Pig? *Writer Girl pushes her hair back and tucks an escaped tendril behind her ear. She is baffled and can't figure out how to include everything in her story. And why, she wonders, is that Eric guy hiding under the table?*

The problem is, when I began to do this writing exercise I started out describing this old woman who collects empty pop cans to supplement her meagre income. In my mind, she lived in an old house with about seventy-five cats so the place was smelly and you couldn't walk in without stepping on empty tuna fish cans. So, I figured I'd find a way to incorporate whatever words I was given into my story. I didn't think I'd have a problem at all with the exercise. I knew how I would describe her tumbledown house and her pot of broken pencils on top of the upright piano she couldn't play any more because of her crippling arthritis and the fact there were always forty cats on the keyboard. In a junky enough house you can include just about anything. At least, that's what I thought until people started throwing out words like *balloons* and *pig*.

My pen twitches over the page like it's just dying to write something, anything, and I start getting this vague idea that maybe a clown promoting a new restaurant gives the old woman a balloon as she trundles her shopping cart past the street corner where he's standing. I've just started to write how she takes the balloon and in the back of my mind I'm beginning to work on the problem of the pig when another girl shouts out a new word: "Sighing."

It's very confusing and I'm sure I'm not doing it right and that my story is the dumbest thing ever written. I doodle a long, scrawling loop up the side of my page and over the top of the little bit I've written. At the end of it I draw a fat, round balloon. Maybe there's some way to combine a couple of words and describe a sighing pig?

"Heather?"

The girl who said "sighing" leans forward, folding herself over her pad of paper, and nods at me.

"What?"

"Your turn. Say a word."

How was I supposed to know that it was my turn to come up with a word? Nobody said anything about going in a particular order. The other pens keep right on scratching away. Only mine is silent and I can't think of a word. Nothing comes to me at all. It's like I'm stuck in time or something and all the insides of my brains have come unglued and are rattling around inside my skull in a big useless jumble.

"Anything that pops into your head," she whispers, her pen not even slowing down as she encourages me.

"Ahhh . . . an . . . an-te-lope. Antelope."

My cheeks flush. What a dopey word. *Antelope*. But nobody laughs. Now what? How am I supposed to use the word *antelope* in my story of the old can-collecting, cat-obsessed woman? Why didn't I say *refund* or *pop bottle*?

What a mistake to join this group! I was doing fine writing on my own. The exercise seems to grind on forever and ever as the others write and write and write and I force a few feeble words out of my pen. Finally, Eric looks at his watch, sits up (but stays down on the floor), and says, "Time!" He waves his pen at all of us like it's a weapon and he's challenging us all to stop, or else. Not that stopping is a problem for me. I lay my arms over my notebook so nobody can see how little I've written.

"I love this exercise," Eric says with a huge grin. "Gets me all loosened up. Ready to write. Ready to rock. In the groove. On the move."

"Shut up, Eric." A girl with shoulder-length black hair kicks him in the side with the soft tip of her red, embroidered slipper.

"Hey," Eric says, oblivious to her request. "Did you guys hear about Mr. Tomlin's Buick?"

Wynd laughs and nods, but the other two girls look blank.

"He skewered it on a forklift!"

"What!?" Sighing Girl's eyes widen. I can't quite picture what happened.

"It's true," Wynd concurs. "He drove his car around the corner too fast at the sawmill and drove—*whap!*—right into the pointy end of a forklift."

Eric looks a little peeved that Wynd stole his punchline.

"Probably drunk," Sighing Girl says. "Remember when he drove off the road near Tanner's Point and got stuck in the mud flats?"

"He was lucky the tide wasn't in," Eric says, "or he'd be a goner. He got lucky again. The prong of the forklift poked out one of the car's headlights, but Mr. Tomlin was fine."

"We don't have all night to gossip," Slipper Girl says.

"Just for that, you go first, Gillian," Eric says, and disappears back under the table.

Gillian is the youngest member of the group—she's twelve. She nudges her red-rimmed, egg-shaped glasses up her nose with the back of her knuckle and flips over the page in her notebook. It's amazing, in the time we've been writing, she's filled nearly two pages! Her story is about a young badger who lives alone with his ailing mother. The other animals really like him and keep giving him inappropriate presents.

"Badger didn't know how to get the balloons into his den. He was afraid his mother would punish him. He was afraid of balloons. He wondered if he could make a balloon animal in the shape of a pig without popping it. Bangs like that were loud in the den. Frightening. His mother collected model pigs. And antelopes. Her favourite . . ."

I sneak a look down at my page as Gillian reads the rest of her story. *Antelope* may have been a dumb word, but she made it fit into her story okay. I wish now I hadn't been so paranoid about coming up with something great. Gillian's story wasn't exactly a world-class prizewinner, but at least she used all the words.

Eric pulls his notebook out from where he left it underneath the table. His effort is about a man who joins the army and then runs away when his battalion invades some hot jungle nation. Eric's voice is loud and melodramatic as he reads.

"Bertrand Carmichael scrambled up into the tree to retrieve the glittering silvery skin of the weather balloon. It would do the trick. He could line his rusting water tank. Life was good . . . a way to store water close to camp and fresh wild pig and roast antelope for dinner."

When he gets to the end of what he has written he says, "This is my favourite part of the writing group. You never know what will come up. What did you write, Wynd?"

Wynd Bell, the girl on the couch beside me, is older than the rest of us. She's fifteen and seems kind of fierce. Her hair is cut in the shape of two giant cheese wedges. Each strand of hair is curled into a tight spiral so her head looks like it's topped off with a pile of corkscrews. There's no way I could be bothered to put that many curls in my hair every morning. It would take forever and the tiny curlers would probably drive me crazy.

At first I thought her name was spelled, W-I-N-D, but then I noticed how Wynd has covered her notebook with letters cut out from newspaper headlines. Her name is spelled out over and over again and the effect is like a big, messy ransom note.

Wynd's writing is strange, not like anything I've ever heard before. She doesn't use sentences, but it's not poetry, either.

11

"Inside her head, explosions—fire-pocked, burned-out, crusty-popcorn-covered sludge balloons out of her jumbled thoughts. She's screaming, 'You lousy pig!!' but she can't remember who she's ripped up, torn out yelling at sighing antelope ideals bounding unreachable into the African sky."

When she's done, she slaps her notebook on the coffee table, sending two organic-gardening magazines slithering to the floor. She glares at us like she dares us to say anything. If I were brave enough to speak up I'd tell her I've never heard anything like her writing before. That doesn't mean I think it's bad—just intense. I'm glad when Sighing Girl clears her throat.

"Sorry, what's your name?" If I don't learn it soon I'll call her Sighing Girl for the rest of my life. My voice is loud in the room, like it's coming from someone else. My legs prickle again. Next time, I'm going to sit on a different seat.

"Willow."

"Willow what?" I'm trying hard to remember as many names as I can. It's not easy to get used to a new place. My family just moved to Tarragon Island this summer. None of the TWYG kids are in grade seven with me.

Willow arches one dark eyebrow. It really stands out because she has the rest of her face blotted with some kind of white powder so she looks extra pale. Thin, black lines have replaced her lips and dark smudges under her eyes remind me of a skull. This effect is made even more pronounced because of the way she has pulled her hair back from her high forehead. I used to see girls like her walking towards Central High School in Toronto. I never imagined I would talk to one of them. Too creepy.

"Willow. Just Willow," she says louder.

"I heard you. I mean, your last name."

12

"She doesn't have one," Eric says as if that closes the matter. He has rolled back under the table. I wonder how clean it is down there.

Everyone has a last name, I want to say, but Willow is talking.

"Those were dumb words," she says.

"You were the one who said *sighing,*" Eric points out. I didn't mind the word *sighing* as much as some of the others. I guess Eric doesn't see his macho hero doing too much of that. "Just read," he says.

So Willow does, in a slow, clear voice. The story takes place on a barge and then sort of turns into a version of Noah's Ark with two pigs, two antelopes, and a couple of flatworms.

"Gross," Wynd comments.

"No criticism of the free-writes," Eric's voice says from the floor.

"I'm not criticizing. I'm expressing an emotional response."

"Heather—did you write anything?" Gillian peers at me over her notebook. The outside of the notebook is decorated with pictures of wolves.

I was hoping to meet some other young writers when I joined this group. It looks like I've stumbled on a nest of freaks.

"I don't think I want to read."

I'm not usually shy about my writing, but my pitiful effort is hardly something to read aloud, even if there is a rule about not criticizing.

"It's okay," Willow says. "For the first time or two you don't have to read anything aloud—until you get used to us."

"But if you want to stay, you have to participate or you're history." Wynd is a lot less diplomatic than Willow.

"We're not being mean," Eric adds quickly. He's standing beside Gillian and I can see how tall he is.

Skinny as a beanpole, Writer Girl quips.

"It's just that we're all pretty serious about our writing so you probably wouldn't have a good time if you didn't at least try."

He sounds like he's talking to a little kid who doesn't know the first thing about writing. I do know about taking writing seriously. I love to write. I do it every day. I'm working on a novel about a girl who discovers she can see into the future and she can't decide whether that's a good thing or not.

I don't say anything, though. Now my eyes are staring at the magazines spread out like a brightly coloured fan on the table. *Bigger Tomatoes—No Pesticides!* one headline promises.

Writer Girl slides her notebook into her black canvas bookbag and casually checks her watch. Gillian tucks her wolf notebook into a backpack and then takes off her red slippers. These she zippers into the outside pocket of her heavy-duty, covered with pins and bulging with books, pack. When she lets go of the zipper after closing the bag, she rubs the tip of her thumb against her forefinger three times. Writer Girl stands and slowly leaves the room, hoping furiously her mother is waiting outside in the car so she doesn't have to spend another minute with these weirdos.

Chapter Two

Collected Quote #3
There are only two or three human stories, and they go on repeating themselves as fiercely as if they had never happened before.—Willa Cather

"How did it go, pumpkin?"

My mom can't wait to hear all about my first writing group meeting. She's a vet and doesn't have an artistic bone in her body. I think that's why she married my dad. He's an artist, too—only he paints pictures instead of making up stories. My guess is that Mom likes being around creative people because she's so straightforward and practical.

"Fine, I guess. We did a free-writing exercise and the other kids read stuff they'd been working on."

"What are the other kids like?"

Freaks. But aloud I say, "Interesting. Eric, he's fourteen, he writes mysteries. He's pretty good, I guess, but bossy. One girl, Wynd, read part of a story set some time in the future after a plague kills everyone— well, almost everyone—except a few survivors who start this colony where everyone worships rocks. And there's Willow. She read about vampires and stuff." I don't mention that she looks like a vampire herself.

"Wind and Willow? Those are auspicious names for writing group members, don't you think?"

"W-Y-N-D. There's also a girl who writes about

animals—wolves. Her name is Gillian. The animals talk."

The beams of the headlights spray over the trees as we head down our driveway.

"Well, the group sounds quite wonderful!" Sometimes my mom's enthusiasm is hard to take.

"So, how's Matt's science project going?" I ask to distract her.

Mom laughs. "We blew it up after dinner. It was excellent—steam, foam, sparks, smoke."

Matt and Mom have been working on this crazy volcano project for weeks. I can just imagine the mess! Matt's nine. He loves explosions. "So, where did you blow it up? In the kitchen?"

"Actually, we did it out in the garage. But, since you mentioned the kitchen . . ."

I groan. This is not the direction I'd planned for the conversation to take.

"The bad news is there are a few dishes to put away. The good news is I've made your lunch already. It's in the fridge."

Mom's tone of voice is quick and to the point now that she's shifted into super-organized-mother mode. "Oh, and the laundry is in the dryer—if you could take it out and fold everything nicely, that would be a big help. I have an early surgery booked tomorrow and I haven't quite finished writing up my case notes from today. I don't want to get to bed too late."

What about me? I want to ask. Doesn't she know how important it is to get a good sleep on a school night? I hate folding laundry.

"Heather? Are you listening to me?"

"Yes, Mom."

Mom has the only vet practice on Tarragon Island. Her new partner, Dr. Brian deBoer, works part-time because his wife just had a new baby. That's why

Mom is usually the one on call at night and on the weekends. She has always kept pretty strange hours. It's not unusual for Mom to be doing paperwork long after I'm in bed. I wish Dad had come to pick me up. He doesn't expect full reports on my activities. I wonder if Mom could tell that I'm not thrilled with my new group. I wonder if she's disappointed.

"Oh, I nearly forgot. You'll have to watch Matt after you get home from school tomorrow because I've agreed to give a little talk to the poultry farmers about egg binding in young hens."

I guess she's not disappointed. She's too busy. She stops talking as she finds the darkened entrance to our driveway and my thoughts return to the kids in my writing group. They are just plain bizarre—nothing at all like my friends who were in my writing group when my family used to live in Toronto. Maggie and the others back home were normal people who liked to write. I try not to think about Mags and Toronto too much. Thinking about the way my life used to be makes me too sad.

"Sweet dreams, Heather. And don't forget the laundry," is the last thing Mom says to me when we walk into the house. The door to her office closes behind her. I quickly fold the clean clothes and when the last of the socks have been paired and sorted I head for my room to get ready for the morning.

Writer Girl's forehead wrinkles with concentration as she carefully packs her bag for school. She loathes the early morning ride to town on the school bus; too many noisy people with nothing to say to her. She slips her copy of The Lion, the Witch, and the Wardrobe *alongside her math textbook. If all else fails, she knows her favourite book will provide a much-needed distraction.*

Since the voice in my head shuts up when I'm

sleeping, I'm quite happy to crawl into bed the minute I've organized my things.

Writer Girl pulls the soft eiderdown quilt up under her chin and settles in to count pigs, antelopes, and big, red balloons to help her fall asleep.

My brother, Matthew, and I sit silently at the breakfast table. The bottom lids of his eyes are all red and sore, like pink-rimmed rabbit eyes. We both poke at the floating gobs of golden-yellow corn cereal in the bowls in front of us. Neither of us can eat.

At our house, it's not unusual for the phone to ring in the middle of the night—animals don't wait until civilized hours to have their babies or get in accidents. Usually, Mom slips out of the house and tends to the problem. She only bothers to tell us what happened if the case is particularly interesting.

If I hear the phone at all during the night, I ignore her voice as she gives instructions or makes an appointment for the next day, or in real emergencies, the click of the screen door catching when she leaves to make a house call.

Last night, though, was different. Long after the phone rang, my mother's voice murmured on and on. I thought she was giving someone very involved instructions or something but then I heard Dad's voice—and then my mother's voice again, rising, louder and louder until it sounded like she was crying.

I couldn't understand why on earth she would be so upset over a calving Guernsey or a dog that had been hit by a car. Mom is not a weeper. She's used to being the one who holds people's hands when they come into the clinic to get their old, sick cats put to sleep. She stays calm even when animals are terrified or in terrible pain—pain so bad the animals are out of their minds and try to bite or scratch her.

Last night, though, I knew something really serious was going on.

My parents' voices wove in and out of each other, low, anxious, intense. I heard Dad make a phone call.

". . . arrange to come . . . difficult . . . definitely . . . I understand . . . I'm sorry."

Why Dad was talking to one of Mom's patients was beyond me. Why was Mom crying instead of talking to whoever was on the phone?

It seemed like hours and hours that I was lying half asleep in the dark trying to make sense of what was going on, when my eyes snapped open and I was suddenly wide awake. The phone call, my parents' intense, mumbled voices, and my mother's tears had nothing to do with an animal patient.

I crept out of bed and stopped in the doorway of my bedroom. I didn't want to sneak down the hall and then burst into the living room since I could still hear my mother sobbing and my father's voice calm and soothing.

"Shhhh, Bobbi—it's okay. I'm here."

I wanted to know what was going on, but I couldn't move. I strained to hear, to understand, but the only sounds in the quiet house were my mother's sobs.

"Heather?"

I jumped when Matt appeared in the hallway behind me.

"What's happening?"

I took his hand and led him back into his bedroom. We sat side by side on his captain's bed. Tony, our black and white cat, stretched lazily, opened one eye, and went back to sleep.

"Why can't we go down and find out—"

"Shh. Mom's upset."

"Is she sick?"

"I don't think so."

My brain couldn't get organized to make a plan. Beside me in the dark, Matt's whole body tensed and then he let loose with a loud yell. "Dad!"

I pushed him over into his pillow but really, I was glad he had at least done something.

Dad was in Matt's room a moment later. He didn't turn on the light but sat between us on my brother's bed.

"I didn't know you two were awake," he said.

"I heard the phone ring and I . . . I couldn't get back to sleep."

He took my hand in his and put his arm around Matt's shoulders.

"Matthew . . . Heather . . . your grandfather . . ."

Shapes jumped out of the shadows in Matt's room. His kite, suspended from the ceiling in front of his window, loomed large and threatening. I squeezed my eyes shut and heard the heavy thud of Tony jumping off the bed.

"What's wrong with Grandpa?" Matt asked.

Dad didn't say anything. The longer he stayed quiet, the worse I knew the news would be.

"He had a heart attack. It was very sudden."

Our hands squeezed tighter together. Dad's hand was very warm.

"Grandpa's dead?"

There. Matt had said it. I waited for Dad to say, "No, sorry, that's not what I meant. People have heart attacks all the time and get better. He's sick. He's in hospital. He'll get better."

But Dad didn't say any of that. In the dark, he lifted our hands a little off his lap and mumbled, "I'm sorry. Yes. He passed away about an hour ago. There was nothing anyone could do."

He let go of my hand and put his arm around me. Matt kind of gasped when he cried and made squeaky noises like he couldn't breathe. I couldn't move. I just stared at the dark diamond shape of the kite against the window.

Writer Girl froze in the darkness. Froze in the darkness. Froze in the darkness.

I didn't think I would ever move again. *Grandpa dead?* Dad was wrong. There must have been some kind of mistake. Grandpa couldn't be dead because just yesterday I mailed a letter to him in Ontario and he couldn't possibly have received it yet.

The three of us stayed where we were for a long time. Mom didn't come up to join us, though we couldn't hear her any more. She must have shut the door to the living room. Matt finally fell asleep leaning against Dad and then Dad whispered to me that I should go back to my room and try to get a little rest. I don't remember walking down the hall or crawling into my bed. But I must have made the trip and then I must have fallen asleep because the next thing I knew I was in my bed and listening to the clink of breakfast dishes in the kitchen.

"Where's Mom?"

Matt scrubs at his eyes with the back of his hands.

"In bed. I'm taking her some tea and toast," Dad says. He looks awful. His skin is pallid and his eyes are bloodshot. "She'll be out in a bit, Matt. Eat your breakfast."

Matt and I study the unappetizing sludge in our cereal bowls. We don't say anything, but when Dad disappears down the hall towards their bedroom, we both get up and tip our food into the garbage pail. Matt tears off a bit of paper towel and lays it over the sloppy mess so Dad won't notice what we've done. We don't know what else to do after that, so we sit back down at the table and wait.

Dad took one look at me when I came downstairs this morning and said I didn't have to go to school. Since Matt does his lessons at home, he doesn't have to worry about going anywhere, either. The phone rings and I jump up to answer it before I realize maybe I don't want to know who is on the other end. If it's Granny, I think I'll drop the phone and run. I don't know what I'll say if my grandmother is crying.

It isn't my grandmother, though. It's Milly, Mom's receptionist and helper in the vet clinic.

"Hello, Heather, dear. Tell your dad I got his message and I'll be over as soon as I can. I called Brian, Dr. deBoer, and he'll also be in a little later. He said he can help take care of things for the next few days. Tell your dad not to worry."

I hang up the phone and for a moment there is absolute silence in the house.

Writer Girl moves like she's in a dream, her limbs heavy and awkward. She imagines herself stuck in this moment forever, a tragic figure, her face a mask of grief.

The kitchen door bangs open and Dad comes in with Mia, our Yorkshire terrier, trotting close at his heels. He touches me lightly on the shoulder and then turns to pour himself a cup of coffee. "I'll be out in my studio if you need anything," he says, and leaves again, Mia still right behind him, her dog tags clinking softly.

Later, when Mom finally emerges from her bedroom at about lunchtime, she looks like someone who has been ill for a very long time.

Chapter Three

Collected Quote #95
The telephone is enemy number one. Try not to have one in your work room and train your friends not to call during work hours.—Judith Krantz

Friday is a horrible, black, stupid day. I almost wish I had gone to school instead of hanging around at home watching my whole family fall apart.

Once Mom gets up she alternates between making lists, making phone calls, and doing odd jobs. She can't sit still. Every so often she disappears into her bedroom and closes the door and I hear her sobbing.

It's impossible to know where to find her—she prowls from room to room, picking things up and putting them down again. She starts to iron her black blouse, the one she's going to wear to the funeral, and then the phone rings. Mrs. Harrison who lives on the other side of our neighbours, the Cranwells, is calling to ask if we need anything. Mom hangs up, spots her pruning shears on the counter, and goes outside. Her *snip-snip* is sharp and agitated as she trims the bushes outside the window.

I get up from the kitchen table and finish ironing the blouse. I don't do as good a job as Mom, but she doesn't notice. When she comes back into the house after her spontaneous pruning session is over she stares at the blouse hanging neatly over the chair.

"Did you do that?" she asks.

I nod.

She tugs off her gardening gloves.

"Well, thank you."

Then she drifts out of the kitchen and down the hall. She miscalculates the turn at the end of the hallway and knocks the basket of laundry down the basement stairs, then trots down after it to tidy up. I watch all this like I'm living inside a movie and my family is putting on a show for me.

Every now and then Dad makes an entrance when he comes in for a coffee. He hasn't shaved and his hair spikes out in all directions. He is trying hard to stay calm but isn't managing very well.

"Heather, close the bread bag!" Snap. Snap.

"Matt—close the door behind you!" Snap. Snap. Snap.

"Heather—do you have to sit there like a pudding? Find something useful to do." Snap.

This is not like my dad at all.

"Make your mother a cup of tea. I'll finish packing." Mom has made three different packing lists, but so far, her suitcase is still empty on her bed. She's leaving on the first ferry to Vancouver Island in the morning. From there, she'll fly to Ontario to be with Granny for the funeral.

During the time it takes to heat the kettle, rinse the teapot with hot water, find a tea bag, splash a little milk into the bottom of a mug, and arrange every-thing Mom needs for tea on the table, Mom cruises in and out of the kitchen six times.

"Tea, Mom?"

"Yes. Thanks, that would be great." When she finally comes to roost, she sits awkwardly on the edge of her chair, her knee jiggling up and down. She pours the tea, and then she's off again, pacing through the house, carrying her mug.

"I wish I was there already," she says to my dad when he passes her in the hallway.

Me too, I think. I wish she were gone, too, since she can't seem to find any place in this house where she can just sit and be still.

When she brings a basket full of clean towels upstairs and starts folding all the face cloths neatly in thirds, I get this crazy urge to slap her face like they do in the movies when people are freaking out. I don't know why I don't just get up and leave. But I can't—it's just like when I'm watching a scary movie and I want to look away but I can't—I have to watch and see how, exactly, the green alien is going to slime the unsuspecting space cadet.

Matt is nowhere to be seen. He keeps disappearing out to the barn where he spends ages talking to his Dexter cows, Chelsea and Jinnie. At least as the day goes on he starts taking breaks between his crying fits. This morning he cried more than I thought it possible for any human to cry. Every so often Dad goes outside to find Matt to make sure he's okay.

I wish someone were going with Mom tomorrow morning. Dad says we can't all go to the funeral. It's too expensive for us all to fly back to Ontario. Besides, leaving the farm and all the animals would mean finding someone to live at the house while we were gone. But when I look at Mom picking things up, putting things down, roaming from kitchen to bedroom to office to kitchen, I'm worried what will happen when she has to fasten her seatbelt in the plane. She'll implode.

When Dad comes back into the kitchen from another trip out to see Matt, I can't stand it for another minute. I flee to my room and plop down on the bed. I stay there for the rest of the afternoon, and for once, nobody bothers me or tries to make me come out. For once, I don't feel like getting up, reading, going outside—nothing. I don't even feel like writing in my journal.

Before it's even light on Saturday morning, Dad lugs Mom's suitcase down the stairs and squeezes her hand. I'm up to say goodbye even though it's so early.

"Ready? We should go."

I wrap my arms around Mom's neck and she reaches up to pat me on the back.

"Be good," she says. "I've left you a list of chores to do each day while I'm gone. There's also a list of phone numbers on the fridge in case you need to have more milk delivered or the newspaper goes missing . . . or . . ." She stops herself. She must know we're not likely to need the phone numbers she has so carefully typed up.

Matt is crying when he kisses her goodbye.

"Your father will be back early this afternoon," Mom says. "Milly and Brian should be here any minute. I've rescheduled the appointments Brian can't handle today so you won't have to worry about people languishing in long lineups or anything."

Mom is all businesslike, brisk and proper.

I want them to leave so I look at my watch. "Bye."

"I'll feed the dogs," Matt says as soon as Mom and Dad have finally gone from sight.

"I'll start on the dog runs."

For once we don't fight over the chores. Luckily, there aren't many dogs in the boarding kennel so it doesn't take long to feed everyone and clean the runs. Matt and I are walking down to the barn to feed the cows and chickens when Milly arrives.

Milly reminds me of the farmer's wife in a story-book I used to read about the gingerbread man. She's round and soft and has poofy white hair that floats around her head like a cloud.

"Hi, kids! Need a hand?"

"We're almost done," I say, grateful for the offer. I know she has a little more phoning to do to let Mom's clients know she'll be away for a few days. Away to attend her father's funeral.

Most of the time I just keep busy and don't allow myself to think about Grandpa. Grandpa dying. Grandpa being dead. Gone forever.

Tears sting at my eyes and I turn and trot off towards the barn.

"Wait up!" Matt's only nine and he doesn't like to run. He's one of these people who likes to do every-thing slowly and methodically. He always does his chores in the same order.

I'm the opposite. I get distracted very easily. I slow down to let him catch up and imagine how I can use the idea of someone being easily distracted in a short story. Thinking about a story helps me not think about Grandpa.

Come to think of it, Grandpa was the one who told me the human brain can't think of more than one thing at a time. This makes me think of Grandpa again and this time I can't stop the tears. They splash down my cheeks and it's Matt who can see to open the latch on the barn door to let us into the cool darkness inside.

Tuesday, September 21

Today is Grandpa's funeral. Mom phoned last night. It was strange to hear her voice. She sounded like one of those voices made by a computer. Flat. Hollow—like she was forming words but not understanding them. Or, maybe it was my ears. Maybe I was hearing in a strange way and not understanding. We didn't say much because it was long distance and really late at night in Ontario and it seemed like Mom didn't want to talk anyway. Maybe she wasn't alone. I don't like to talk on the phone when I know someone's listening.

It's not quite lunchtime, so I have a few minutes to try and catch up on my journal. I estimate that with the time difference (it's three hours later in Ontario) people will be arriving at the church in half an hour. Is it sick and morbid that I wish I could be at the funeral? I haven't been back to school since we heard the news but Dad says I have to go back tomorrow. I don't want to go back. Not tomorrow. Not ever. Here's what I would do if I could.

I would go to Narnia, just like Lucy does in <u>The Lion, the Witch, and the Wardrobe</u>. I would push through the coats at the back of an old wardrobe and I would wander through the forest waiting for Mr. Tumnus to appear. He would come trotting through the trees, of course, and the two of us would have tea in a cozy café. It would be so excellent to really meet someone who is half goat and half man. We might even find Lucy in the forest and the three of us could sit at a little table at the café together eating Turkish Delight and discussing how to solve all the problems of the world. It would be just like when Dad and I used to go to our favourite coffee shop in Toronto after we'd spent an afternoon hanging out in bookshops. We'd go to Blinkoes and he'd have a cappuccino and I'd drink steamed milk. In Narnia it would be just like that only better.

Okay, this is dumb. There are no cafés in Narnia.

I close the cover of my journal and slide it into a drawer in my rolltop desk. When I was little I used to be able to imagine that I actually travelled into the worlds of the books I read. But today, sitting in Dove Cottage, my little hideaway where I come to work, imagining myself in Narnia seems babyish beyond belief.

28

I look around at the wooden walls and dirt floor of the old chicken coop Dad and I fixed up in the summer. You'd never know chickens used to live in here or how much work we did to clean the place out. When we'd shovelled out all the chicken manure, we painted the coop a kind of pale purpley colour with black trim around the windows and door. My friend Alyssum from next door helped paint. Mom made some curtains and Granny helped me find the perfect desk. That was in the summer when she and Grandpa came to visit. Dad says it's lucky they had a chance to visit us in our new house before . . . when they did, because now we have memories of Grandpa associated with our little farm on Tarragon Island.

I disagree. To me, it's so sad Grandpa won't ever get to move here like he thought he might. If he hadn't come to see us he wouldn't have known what he was missing. I wonder what he was thinking just before he died? Maybe he was thinking about how he wouldn't get to come here after all.

Thinking about Grandpa when he had his heart attack and imagining that he might have been thinking about how he would never see us again makes me start crying again about how unfair every single thing is. I've just put my head down on my desk to settle in for a good weep when I hear several sets of boots crunching in the gravel of the driveway outside.

My desire to have a good cry fights with my growing curiosity and I pull aside the curtain and peer out. Our neighbours, the Cranwells, have come to visit. Mr. and Mrs. Cranwell live on the farm right next door to ours. Alyssum Cranwell is ten and they also have baby twins, Robert and Eric. I'm not sure what age kids stop being babies and become toddlers, but it seems to me the Cranwell twins are right on the line. They can stand up and stagger a couple of steps before they plop onto their diaper-padded bottoms, but they still nurse and get carried around most of the time. Today, Mr. and Mrs. Cranwell each have one twin in a baby backpack strapped onto their backs. Sandy, their golden retriever, runs ahead of them and stops dead in her tracks when she sees Mia come bounding down the front steps.

Mia bounces up and down yipping wildly and Milly and Matt come out the front door to see what all the racket is about. Mrs. Cranwell says something and Milly nods and points in the direction of Dove Cottage. Alyssum turns and runs back down the steps when the rest of her family disappears inside the house.

I wipe my eyes and let the curtain drop. Quickly, I sit at my desk, pull out a sheaf of papers, and fumble around to find a pen that works so by the time Alyssum arrives at the door, I'm bent over the desk, hard at work.

"Come in," I say as gruffly as I can manage, as if I'm being interrupted.

Alyssum comes in much more quietly than I'm used to (she's usually full of chatter) and says, "Hi."

I'm so taken aback by her subdued entrance that I turn around to see if she's okay.

Alyssum stands just inside the door. She's wearing a long tunic that is several shades of blue. At the top, around her neck, it's very pale, sky blue, and by the time it reaches her feet it is such a dark colour the blue seems almost black. She has a black turtleneck on underneath and the whole outfit makes her look both older and taller than she really is.

"Have a seat," I say, forgetting that I was going to ignore her. Suddenly, I'm really glad she has come to visit.

She plunks herself into the beanbag in the corner and stares up at the ceiling. There's a long pause where neither of us says anything. Finally, she sighs and says, "So, I can talk to you?"

"Of course you can talk to me. What do you mean?"

"My mom said you might be . . . well, in a delicate condition."

A laugh snorts out of me and Alyssum looks shocked. "Delicate condition? Isn't that what they say when someone is pregnant?"

Alyssum's eyes fly open and her hand goes to her mouth. "No! That's not what I meant!"

"It's fine," I say quickly. "I'm fine." That's a lie, but I sure don't want Alyssum treating me like I'm some sort of invalid. "Delicate? Not me." She takes me at my word and relaxes back into the cushioning hollow of the beanbag.

"That's good. Because I need your help."

"My help? Do you have a new project?"

Alyssum home-schools. In fact, that's where my parents got the idea for Matt to study at home, too. Sometimes, Alyssum and Matt get together to work on stuff. Alyssum is really good at starting fantastic projects but not so good at finishing them. It's not the first time she has asked for help getting some complicated thing completed.

"Not exactly. I'm collecting stamps."

I nod. I already know that. Alyssum doesn't collect stamps like a normal person to put them in albums and trade with other people. She collects stamps from people all over Tarragon Island. She has drop-off boxes everywhere—at the little library, the lobby of the post office, at each of the checkouts in the grocery store, and in both the elementary and high schools.

She collects the donations, sorts and bundles them up, and every month or so takes them in to a stamp dealer in Victoria. The dealer buys them and then

Alyssum takes the proceeds and donates them to UNICEF. The money she raises helps children in poor countries to get things like clean drinking water, and pencils and books for school. Alyssum's whole family is into projects like that.

"I need you to help me find out who donated some stamps that were left at the high school."

"What? Why?" I can't imagine why she would want to know where the stamps came from. People just collect the stamps they get in the mail and toss them in the boxes. Sometimes they leave whole envelopes and Alyssum has to tear off the corners with the stamps and then soak the bits of paper in the bathtub until the stamps come off. It's a big job to dry, organize, and bundle all the stamps she gets each month. "Do you want to send a thank-you note or something?"

"Not exactly. Maybe. No, not really."

Alyssum doesn't usually sound so vague. She looks around like she's worried someone might overhear what she has to say and then leans forward to whisper, "I think someone made a mistake."

"What?"

"Someone left some very valuable stamps on the table at the high school."

"That's good, isn't it?"

Her forehead wrinkles. "Maybe. There was this whole set of stamps from Russia—hundreds of them, all mounted on sheets and bound in a plastic folder. I looked some of them up on the Internet and I figure the collection must be worth about five thousand dollars."

"What! Are you sure?"

"Yes, I'm sure. Keep your voice down."

"Who's going to hear? Who's going to care?"

"My parents don't know I have them. Mom said

that if I was going to do a big project like this stamp thing, I had to be responsible for it. I want to figure this out on my own."

"You're not going to keep them, are you?"

"No." She looks disgusted that I would even think such a thing. "But I can't even offer to give them back since I don't know where they came from. I want to find out who donated them—to make sure whoever it was really meant to. I can't just sell them and make a big donation because I'm afraid—"

"Afraid? Why would you be afraid? It's probably just a rich collector who wants to be generous but stay anonymous. There are people like that in the world. They're called philanthropists."

Alyssum is unimpressed with my big word. "I can't donate stamps that valuable. The stamp shop in Victoria, or the people at UNICEF, might think I stole them."

This possibility hadn't occurred to me.

"Or, if the owner discovers he or she donated the wrong stamps by mistake and I sell them, then I'll owe five thousand dollars which I will already have donated to UNICEF. That would be awful! So, you see, if you could find out who made the donation, I could phone them up and ask if they really wanted to do it."

"Don't you think if someone had made a mistake they would have discovered it by now and called you up? Everybody on this island knows you are the girl who collects stamps."

"I thought of that. Maybe the collector is on vacation or doesn't sort through their stamps very often and doesn't realize they're missing."

"And anyway," I interrupt, "how am I supposed to find out who made the donation?"

"Can't you ask around at school to see if anyone

saw who left stamps on the table last week?"

"But I wasn't even at school the whole time! Besides, lots of people drop off stamps."

"But not everyone leaves a donation in a Tamolinos' Secrets box. Shoe boxes, yes. Plastic bags, yes. Big envelopes, all the time. But nobody's ever left an underwear box full of stamps before."

Tamolinos' Secrets is a fancy boutique in Victoria that sells very expensive ladies' underwear and pyjamas.

"There were so many stamps they wouldn't all fit in my donation box, so whoever it was left the Russian stamps in their own box."

"How is that going to help me?"

"Maybe the secretary or someone saw a person with a Tamolinos box."

It seems like a long shot to me, but since Alyssum seems so worried, I agree to ask around.

"Be careful," she adds, her face all scrunched up again. "If it is someone really rich who wants to be anonymous, I sure don't want to offend them in case they want to make more big donations."

How on earth I'm supposed to ask questions without letting anyone know I'm investigating the mysterious stamps is beyond me. And thinking about school reminds me how much I don't want to go back.

"You're so lucky you don't have to go to school."

"Hmmmm . . ." Alyssum groans. "Not really. I can't get my crystals to grow and Mom has made me do my science experiment three times over. At school, I could just get a C and get on with something else. Mom doesn't care so much about the grades—she cares about doing stuff right."

She sighs like this is the biggest pain in the world.

"Alyssum?"

Mr. Cranwell's voice calls from somewhere outside.

"Don't tell your parents, okay? About the stamps, I mean. When it's all over, after I've found the owner of the stamps, I'll tell Mom and Dad everything. I want my mother to know I can handle my responsibilities."

She sounds so serious it's hard not to laugh.

"Still, it might not be a bad idea to . . ."

Alyssum doesn't give me a chance to finish. She scoots out the door and runs back to the house where her parents and brothers are already getting ready to leave. They head down the driveway and then a few minutes later there's another knock at Dove Cottage.

"Heather?"

"Come in," I say, and Dad ducks inside.

"The Cranwells came to bring a casserole and see how we're doing."

"That was nice," I say.

"The food is still warm—are you ready to come in for lunch?"

I shrug. I haven't felt much like eating for the past few days, especially if it's meant bothering to make something for myself.

"Come on inside, pumpkin—I need you and Matt to give me a hand tidying up so the place is reasonable when your mother gets home tomorrow. Milly could also use a hand with the little guys."

We keep small animals in one of the rooms at the vet clinic—rodents and birds, and occasionally reptiles. Most of the "little guys" are boarders, but sometimes Mom keeps an animal that needs a new home. These "temporary" guests can wind up staying for months until Mom finds a suitable adoptive family. I can tell my time alone in Dove Cottage is over for the time being, so I follow Dad inside.

Chapter Four

Collected Quote #20
Writing is my vacation from living.—Eugene O'Neill

"Hi, Heather," Milly says. "Are you going to help me with the little guys?"

We don't have many small creatures at the clinic at the moment—a long-haired guinea pig called Widget, Benjamin and Disraeli, a pair of rats, and Snow, a white budgie.

When Milly and I walk into the room, Widget lets out a piercing whistle. Snow runs along her perch and pokes her head up inside a swinging bell. She peeks out for a second to make sure we've noticed her and then sticks her head back up into the bell.

Milly and I can't help ourselves—we both crack up.

"Snow—you little ham!"

Snow bends her legs, bobs her head, pings at the bell with her beak, and then hops down to her food dish.

I hear myself giggling. It's weird, like I've caught myself lying or something. I blush and the laugh withers in my throat. It's not right to laugh when someone dies.

"It's okay, Heather." Milly touches my shoulder and then turns to talk to the budgie. "Snow, you are a very funny bird. Shall we give you some salad?"

"Salad" for Snow consists of lettuce, a tiny bit of pasta, a few peas, and some chopped-up apple. She's a greedy little thing and digs right in when I snap the feeding dish back into her cage. She flips bits of lettuce aside and flings them to the bottom of the cage. A piece of apple catches her eye and she munches away happily.

I'm not generally a bird person, but Snow has such a cool personality I can almost imagine having a pet like her.

Milly and I zoom through the cages and it doesn't take long at all before the little critters have fresh bedding, clean water, and bowls full of food.

Wednesday, September 22—Midnight

I'm having a lot of trouble sleeping these days. Grandpa's funeral was yesterday. Mom is coming home tomorrow. She has been away nearly a whole week but it still feels like last night was the night I heard the phone ring.

I went back to school today. Emma Patten is in my homeroom. I met her once before at the Saturday market. She's pretty nice, I guess. She has another friend, Briony. They mostly hang out together. Everybody keeps looking at me funny, with pity or something. In Toronto it was easy to have secrets. It's not so easy here. I don't feel like talking to people about my private life, so I said I had a cold. Of course, nobody believed me.

I snuck out of the house and brought a candle out here to Dove Cottage. The candle light turns my page yellow and flicker paints the shadowy corners pitch black. I'm glad I thought to bring Mia with me because otherwise I would be scared. Not that there's anything to be scared of—just that it's dark and a little spooky out here and if I screamed nobody would hear me because they're in the house sound asleep.

The reason why I came out here in the middle of the night is I was lying in bed, staring at the outline of my bookcase and all of a sudden it popped into my head that I still haven't done my homework assignment for the writing group tomorrow. I was going to work in my room

37

but then I realized I'd left my notebook out here and by this point I was so wide awake I figured I might as well get dressed and come outside.

I wasn't even going to go back to the group so I wasn't worried about my homework, but earlier today when I was out here, Dad came to visit. Talk about bad timing. He said in his really sensitive voice, "You don't have to go to the writer's group tomorrow if you don't want to. I understand how you are feeling." Right then I was making a list of all Grandpa's favourite sayings in my journal so I won't forget. I'd just written down, "When the going gets tough, the tough get going." So I said, "I'm fine. It's important to keep going even when something bad happens."

Dad looked sort of surprised and then he smiled and nodded. He said that was very mature of me.

So, by my own stupidity I will have to go to at least one more meeting and that means I have to do my homework. Each week, a different person in the group assigns some sort of writing project for us to do.

Next week I'll tell Dad I'm quitting.

I sigh and lean back in my chair. Writing about my problems in my journal is not helping get my assignment done. No matter what, I'm not going to more than one more meeting of the dumb group. I'll explain to the group why I'm not coming back. I'll have to make up a good excuse, but I'm sure that won't be hard once I get there and am reminded of what a bunch of weirdos they all are.

Since I've so cleverly talked Dad into letting me go tomorrow and I'm doing my assignment, they aren't likely to tease me or kick me out. Though it would be easier in some ways if they would ban me from the group—then I wouldn't have to give them a reason for quitting.

Outside, there's a noise like someone shuffling through the grass and my pen freezes over the page.

Though I can't see beyond the yellow pool of light of my candle, I stare at the wall of Dove Cottage like if I stare hard enough the wall will disappear and I'll be able to see what's out there.

Mia lifts her head and tilts it from side to side. I hear another noise outside and my heart races so fast I think it might explode. Strange shadows jump and sway over the walls. Mia licks her lips and whines and then puts her head back down on her paws. She stares hard at the door.

"What is it, girl?" I ask her like we're in some kind of Lassie movie and she's going to save me from . . . from whatever danger lurks just outside the door.

Something, or someone, touches the doorknob. I see it shifting a little from side to side. I've always wondered what I would do if I were in real danger and now I know—nothing. I can't move. The doorknob twists a little this way and a little that way and I want to scream "Well open the door and come on in and put me out of my misery!" My mouth, though, won't work. I'm so terrified I discover I'm not even breathing.

Mia gets up and sticks her nose to the crack at the bottom of the door. I want to jump up and pull her back out of harm's way. Then her tail starts to wag slowly from side to side.

Dogs are supposed to sense danger, right? So, if she's not howling her head off or cowering under the desk, whatever it is out there can't be too, too dangerous. Right?

"Mia, who's out there?" I ask her more insistently, like she might really answer me if I am firm enough. Instead, she backs away from the door, turns three times in place, and lies down again on the floor near my chair. I look back at the door handle thinking maybe I imagined it all, that it was just the shadowy light playing a trick with my eyes, when the knob moves again.

Before I can think, I jump out of my chair and yank the door open, fully expecting to see Matt there, trying to scare me. Instead, it is Mathilde, our tortoiseshell cat, who strolls in nonchalantly, her tail straight up in the air, her amber eyes gleaming.

"You silly cat!"

She jumps up on my desk, sits right on top of the open page of my journal and licks her paw. Paying no attention whatsoever to me or the dog, she draws her paw up behind her ear and proceeds to thoroughly wash her face.

I sit back down in my chair and try to remember what on earth I was thinking about before I was so rudely interrupted. The writing assignment.

This week we are supposed to choose a character in a story we're working on and then write a scene where that character opens a drawer. We have to describe what's in the drawer, I guess, and maybe why our character needs whatever is in there. In my story of the orphan girl who can see into the future, the main character runs away from an orphanage in Toronto. She winds up on a farm living with two kind old people who take pity on her.

At least, that's what the novel used to be about. I haven't worked on it all week because in my mind the farm I was basing the book on was my grandparents' farm near Guelph and the old people were a lot like Granny and Grandpa. The problem is, every time I think about their farm I want to cry, and in the book the farm is supposed to be a happy place. A sanctuary.

The Tarragon Island Composite High School is

pathetic. We only have one class for each grade from seven to twelve. In total, maybe two hundred kids attend classes, and that includes kids who arrive by boat each morning from some of the smaller islands nearby. The high school in Toronto I would have attended if we hadn't moved has nearly two thousand students and an indoor swimming pool.

Here on Tarragon Island, the teachers all wear thick wool sweaters and have beards—well, except for the women. They wear hiking boots and pull their long hair back with clips made out of bits of bone and driftwood.

Okay, maybe only Miss Carlton, the art teacher, looks exactly like that, but the rest of them probably think that way.

The worst part about my new school is the dumb buddy system they dreamed up. Steffie Andropov was assigned to be my buddy. Steffie is part of the ultra-cool crowd. She, Alicia, Terri, and Su have posters of movie stars plastered all over their lockers. Yesterday at lunch they spent the entire hour painting cute little flowers over the top of their silvery nail polish.

Puke. What a waste of time. This is how the conversation went:

Steffie: Ooooooh! I love this sparkly green!

Alicia: Yeah . . . it's, like, excellent.

Steffie: That's so cool. You're, like, such a good artist.

(Steffie said that because Su drew this teeny, tiny spider on Alicia's pinky fingernail.)

Su: Not really. I'm bad at art.

Alicia: No way—you're really good.

Su: Not really.

Alicia: Yes really.

Su: Forget it.

Steffie: Do one for me when my base is dry, okay?

I can't believe that anyone can spend a whole hour talking about nail polish and denying they're good at anything. Then, I made a total fool of myself when Terri asked if I wanted my nails done and I said, "No thanks. I'm allergic."

Mistake.

"Nobody is allergic to nail polish!" Alicia started laughing her head off. Instead of keeping my mouth shut, I tried to prove it was true.

"As a matter of fact, it's a rare condition called . . . chemical hypersensitivity disease."

"As a matter of fact? Yeah, right." Though Alicia didn't look quite so sure of herself after that.

"I think I've heard of that," Su said. "So are you allergic to soap and stuff, too?"

"No." I don't actually know anything about chemical sensitivity and I'm certainly not allergic to anything that I know of.

"I don't have it very badly," I said. "Only to things with very strong smells like nail polish and . . . some felt pens."

I knew even as I said it that I was going to regret lying.

"How about cigarette smoke?" Steffie pulled a pack of cigarettes from her bag. She glanced back towards the school to see if any teachers were around. There weren't, so she lit up.

"As a matter of fact, yes—I am highly sensitive to smoke."

"As a matter of fact, I figured you would be," Steffie said, mocking me. She passed the cigarette to Su who had a puff before passing it on to Alicia. Their nails glistened in the sun and as each girl took a drag she left a slightly different shade of lipstick on the filter.

"Where did you get these?" Alicia asked.

Steffie's lips moved as she inspected the contents of the packet, counting.

"Took them from my brother's sports bag. There's almost a full pack! He can't tell on me because Mom and Dad would kill him for smoking." She threw her head back melodramatically. "It's such a pain that our local source is so unreliable."

I wonder who on earth Steffie's source might be. It's not easy to buy cigarettes if you're underage. I can't imagine what the school was thinking when they picked Steffie to be my buddy. Not only do we have nothing in common, the kids who might be interesting as friends won't have anything to do with the cool crowd. It's like these people live in two completely different worlds.

In one world you know all the words to the latest Hi-Bar song, you're on a diet, have a boyfriend (though I've never seen any of the so-called boyfriends come closer than twenty paces), and the colour of your hair clips matches your socks. If you happen to be in the other world (Steffie and Co. refer to non-cool people as weasel-bugs) you chew your nails, do your homework on time, and wear buttons with messages like "Free Captive Whales!"

And then, there's me. I don't belong to either group. I think it would be easier to get accepted by Steffie and Co. because at least I know their rules. It's already too late to start smoking because of my so-called chemical condition, but it would help if I could say I have a boyfriend. That would go a long way towards counteracting the damage of being allergic to nail polish and felt pens.

Chapter Five

Collected Quote #35
Some reviews give pain. This is regrettable, but no author has the right to whine. He was not obliged to be an author. He invited publicity, and he must take the publicity that comes along.—E.M. Forster

Charlene Opens a Drawer

It's impossible to open the drawer of the old oak bureau without making a noise. Inside the drawer is where Charlene keeps her collection of crystal balls. She has fourteen of them—all sizes. So they don't break when they roll back and forth, she has wrapped them in silk scarves so they make a kind of muffled rumble when they move.

I finish reading my homework assignment aloud and lean back on the wooden chair. It's really hard to concentrate since Mom only got back from Ontario this afternoon and everything seems very strange at our house. Mom walks around like she has her head stuffed with cotton wool. She says she's really tired after the trip. I had to repeat that tonight was my writing group and I needed a ride three times before the information sank in. I would ride my bike to the meetings except Mom and Dad say it's not safe to ride on the narrow island roads after dark. Dad is trying to make things easy for Mom so she doesn't have to worry about anything and that's why he drove me tonight.

Matt acted really weird. When Mom walked in he started following her around like he was scared she would disappear if he let her out of his sight.

All of this flies through my head as I'm waiting for someone to say something about my assignment.

"That's not bad," Eric says like he's being kind and generous but really thinks it's awful. "But if you're trying to build suspense, you could do a lot to make it more mysterious." For a change, he's kneeling on a cushion on the floor beside the coffee table.

"Hey, Mr. Know-it-all, you don't know everything about suspense," Wynd says from where she's sprawled on the couch. She has it to herself this evening. I guess nobody else can stand to get prickled. "Has it ever occurred to you she might not be writing a mystery?"

"Yeah, it occurred to me. Mysteries are too hard for most people."

Eric ducks down behind the table when Wynd whips her pen at him. The pen skids across the floor and disappears under the radiator. Eric crawls over and fishes it out. "Did you drop this?" He passes the pen back with a smirk and then looks at me. "My point is just that she might not want to say right away what's making the noise in the drawer."

Willow stretches first one leg and then the other as she unfolds herself from her yoga position on the floor. Her black cape is spread in a circle around her and she's sitting plumb in the middle of it like some gothic princess.

"I agree with Eric. Not that you couldn't write mysteries, Heather, that's not what I mean." She turns her serious gaze to Eric and says, "You aren't *that* good, you know. But, I agree with you about keeping the reader guessing. If Heather didn't say right away

45

what was making the noise, we'd think it was maybe skulls or something."

"Skulls?" Wynd sniffs. "Personally, I think the whole thing is kindov lame. Orphans have been done to death, you know?"

"She could hear coconuts rolling around in the drawer, maybe," Gillian says softly.

"Coconuts? Come on—that's way beyond lame."

"Wait, wait, wait. We're not supposed to say how she has to fix it," Eric says. "We're supposed to make helpful suggestions."

I guess nobody can think of anything helpful because suddenly everyone is very intent on staring at something other than me.

"I'm not saying she has to change anything—and I never said I was the only one here who can write mysteries. My point was that the story might be more powerful, more gripping, if she made a few adjustments."

I feel like I'm shrivelling up as I listen to the others hack my writing to pieces as if I'm not even in the room. I force myself to guide my pen to form the words, *gripping* and *skulls*? and *coconuts*? so it looks like I'm taking notes. I wonder how long the critiquing part lasts.

"What doesn't make sense to me," Wynd says, "is how on earth an orphan got hold of a bunch of crystal balls and silk scarves. Did she steal them?"

Writer Girl raises her gold-nibbed fountain pen as if to use it like a wand to punctuate a profound comment. She considers the possibility that it might not be altogether believable for Charlene to have all those crystal balls. She nods wisely, appreciative of the thoughtful suggestions offered by her peers. Writer Girl is not one to feel wounded by suggestions—not when the end result is sure to be a novel of considerable literary merit.

I ignore my burning eyes and force myself to consider the crystal ball point. Unfortunately, Wynd isn't finished. "If I was reading a book like that I'd close it when I got to that part and not read another word."

Tears spring to my eyes. It feels like Wynd punched me in the stomach. The theory of accepting constructive criticism is much easier than the practice.

"Do you want more feedback?" Willow asks.

"No. I mean, thanks for your input. I . . . I made some notes. Do I have to bring it back after I make some changes?" I can't imagine going through the agony of the feedback grinder again.

"It's up to you," Willow says.

"Yeah—it just depends how serious you are about improving," Eric says and fishes his notebook from his backpack. Even though he's fourteen, he looks like he's only about ten. It doesn't help that he dresses like a skateboarder and even when he's at the writing group he never takes off his elbow and knee pads. He's in grade eight at my school. He doesn't seem to think much of Steffie and Co., though a couple of times he's nodded to me in the halls when I've been alone.

When Eric reads his homework assignment the hairs on my arms tingle. By the time he gets to the part where his main character, Brock Carrington, opens the drawer, I'm literally on the edge of my seat and holding my breath. When Brock reaches into the drawer to pull out the broken knife blade, I'm ready to yell out, "Stop! Don't do it!"

Of course, I keep my mouth shut—even when Eric closes his notebook and everyone else begins to critique. Compared to what they said about mine, their comments about Eric's work are gentle.

"That was great!" Gillian says. "I wouldn't change a thing!"

"Maybe describe the room a little more?" Willow offers, but then changes her mind. "Maybe not. The creaky floor and the smells of tobacco and gunpowder actually add enough to the atmosphere."

"What about readers who have never smelled gunpowder?" Wynd asks.

"They can use their imaginations," Eric says. "You can't spell too much out or it gets boring."

I think it's getting boring that Eric thinks he knows everything there is to know about writing mysteries.

"What about you? What do you think, Heather?"

I know Willow is just trying to include me, but I wish she'd leave me alone. I want to say, "Fantastic!" but I'm too annoyed with Eric to lavish that much praise on his work, so instead I say, "I guess I liked it."

It's vague and dumb and probably not very helpful but there's something about the kids in this group (and particularly Eric) that makes me feel totally tongue-tied and foolish.

"How's the novel going?" Wynd asks Eric when it's clear I'm not going to say anything else.

Eric grins and bobs his head up and down. His quick movement reminds me of Snow, the perky white budgie. For the next few minutes he tells us all about how he is looking for ways to make his villain, Alfonso Mendoza, likeable so the reader gets tricked into feeling sympathetic. Despite myself, I like what he's saying. Eric might be a snotty little jerk, but he really does take his writing seriously.

Suddenly he cuts off and looks straight at me. "Heather, you said you were working on a novel, too. How's it going?"

For the life of me I don't know why I say what I do.

Maybe it's because I was inspired by the way everyone was so caught up in Eric's story. Or maybe because I'm an idiot and sometimes speak before I think.

"I was thinking that I might like to change it into a mystery."

"Really?"

I can't tell if Eric is pleased, or what. There's a strange stir in the others and then a terrible silence.

"Well . . . I was thinking—" It's very hard to come up with something since I hadn't been thinking at all. "I was thinking it might make the story more interesting if Charlene discovers something mysterious at the farm."

"A body?"

Eric leans forward, his eyes bright. He's really listening to me now.

"Yeah. A body."

"In the barn or something?"

"I guess so."

Eric scribbles something on a blank page in his notebook and then tears it out and gives it to me.

"It's the title of a great reference book about solving murders—what police investigators do. You can order it through the bookstore. You'd probably find it useful. Have you met Mitch yet? He owns the bookstore."

Eric doesn't wait for me to answer. "He's actually William O'Donnell. I mean, Mitch is his real name. His pen name is William O'Donnell."

"O'Donnell? You mean the novelist? The one who writes those lawyer crime books?"

"Same guy. He's not at the store all the time, but when he's there he's great to talk to because he knows everything about writing."

"He lives on a schooner at Bigelow's Marina," Willow adds.

"With his fourth wife Bunny," Wynd chips in.

"And seven or eight cats," Gillian says.

"It probably stinks on that boat," Wynd says.

"Is any of this relevant to Heather?" Willow asks.

"We're just helping her get to know her neighbours," Eric says.

How on earth will I ever get to know everyone on this island the way the locals do?

"Order that book," Eric says firmly. "You'll find it useful."

It's impossible to know whether Eric is trying to be helpful or whether the note is really a put-down because he thinks I obviously don't know anything about crime investigations. Which I don't.

"Thanks."

"You're welcome."

The awkward politeness of the moment passes when Gillian clears her throat and asks if she can start reading. As she launches into the next part of her story about the wolf pack, I feel like I've been tricked. Eric probably wants me to try my hand at a mystery novel just so he can show off how much better he is at writing them. Not only that, I can't think how to graciously announce that I'm quitting the group now that everyone is expecting to hear me read some crime investigation scene at the next meeting.

I lean back on the wooden chair, close my eyes, and pretend to listen carefully to Gillian's story. In truth, I have to concentrate very hard to keep from bursting into tears.

On the way home, Dad is lost in his own thoughts and doesn't speak until we get to the end of our driveway.

"Quiet when we go in—your mother went to bed early."

"Early surgery?"

He pauses for a minute. "No. She was just tired. Long trip."

I'm so distracted thinking about how dumb my orphan story is and wondering how on earth I'm going to find a plausible reason for a dead body to show up in the barn that Dad's words don't sink in.

"Heather?"

"What." I guess I must have sounded just a little grumpier than I meant to because Dad glares at me and says, "Watch your tone of voice."

"Sorry."

"I just wanted to say your mother has been through a lot. I need you to . . . well, do what you can to help."

The dead body in the barn, the dumb writing group, my new homework assignment, all those pictures that had been so bright in my head just a moment ago fade away like the edge of a dream as it recedes before the glare of the morning sun.

I'm not sure what Dad wants me to do, though it doesn't feel like he's in a mood to have a long discussion about it.

"Okay." Under my breath I add, *Whatever*, and then look over at him to see if he heard my thought. Of course, he hasn't noticed anything. He sighs and nods, his eyes fixed straight ahead, watching the dark, winding road.

We drive the rest of the way home in silence.

One of the things I'm trying to train myself to do is to keep thinking about my stories no matter what else is going on around me. It's a kind of challenge I've set for myself. When Dad and I walk into the kitchen my thoughts are back to churning around the mess I'm in with my novel and I'm feeling kind of smug that even though I'm tired and a little worried about Mom, I can still focus on Charlene who, at this point anyway, is still an orphan.

Matt is sitting at the kitchen table in front of a golden-brown apple cake. The top of the cake is drizzled with white icing.

"Want some?" he asks.

I can't understand my brother. He loves to bake and cook but he doesn't cheat and snack without sharing. If I baked a cake, half of it would be gone before anyone even had a chance to see it.

"Smells good!" Dad says and gives Matt's shoulder a squeeze. "Your mother didn't want any before bed?"

Matt's apple cake is one of Mom's all-time favourite desserts.

"Nope. She said she wasn't hungry."

We all stare at the cake as if it's alive.

"All the more for us," Dad jokes and reaches for a plate. Somehow, his words just aren't funny and though the cake is delicious, I can't finish my whole piece. Not only that, every shred of my concentrate-on-my-story-at-all-costs-self-discipline has evaporated. Instead, all my thoughts are filled with Mom and how very strange it feels that she isn't sitting at the table with us cracking jokes, planning explosions with Matt, or telling us a story about rescuing an injured baby squirrel from some terrified old lady's chimney.

Cake, I decide as I push my plate back, is just no good without the proper conversation for flavouring.

Chapter Six

Collected Quote #109
My mother groan'd! my father wept,
Into the dangerous world I leapt.—William Blake

At school the next day I go to the office and wait patiently in line while people fill in late slips and hand in lunch order forms. Steffie and the other girls expected me to run to the store with them at recess, but I said I had to go to the library to take out a couple of books for the socials assignment I missed. I hope they don't come back early and see me in the office instead. When it's finally my turn to talk to Mr. Bell, the school secretary, I'm already bright pink and the narrative in my head is galloping along at full tilt.

Writer Girl runs her fingertip along the grain of the wooden counter in the school office, tracing the wriggling cracks as if she's planning a journey on a relief map. The man behind the desk seems vaguely familiar, something about the way he stares at her like she's intruding.

"You know the stamp drop-off box?" I stutter.

Mr. Bell nods and glances up at the clock on the wall behind me. I know the bell is about to ring to signal the end of recess so I talk faster.

"Did you happen to notice if anyone brought some stamps in a Tamolinos box?"

Mr. Bell lifts one bushy eyebrow. "Tamolinos' Secrets? Isn't that the . . . the shop where women buy

53

their dainties?"

Now Mr. Bell looks distinctly uncomfortable. *Dainties*? The funny, old-fashioned term nearly makes me giggle out loud.

"Yes. That's the place."

"I thought people put donations in the shoebox Alyssum left over there on the table."

"Well, yes. That's what they're supposed to do. But someone had a lot of stamps and they left them in a Tamolinos box."

I can see the next question forming in his mind even before his lips begin to move.

"Why do you need to know who left the stamps?"

My mouth opens and I cough because I can't think of a good answer right away. "Alyssum found a . . . a . . . letter in the box that she thinks the person might have left in there by accident."

"Isn't there an address on the envelope?"

For a moment, I'm stumped and my ears burn hotly. "No. I mean, there's no envelope—that's the whole problem. And the first page of the letter is missing so she doesn't even have the first name. Well, never mind. She just thought the person might have wanted to keep the letter, that's all. It doesn't really matter. Thanks."

The buzzer sounds and I nod and back out of the office. I rush off down the hall to math class, the conversation replaying itself in my head. Who would even notice someone dropping off stamps? The table where Alyssum's box sits is right near the office in the front hall. Every student at the school passes the table at least four times a day and every visitor—parents, delivery people, janitors—comes in and out of the front door.

I settle in at my desk and avoid Steffie's glare. For a

moment I feel guilty about the library fib. But Steffie and her group are not the kind of people who are interested in collecting stamps or helping the poor. I don't know how I could have explained my conversation with Mr. Bell.

When Mr. McGuire says, "Now have a look at page forty-seven in your textbook," I turn away from Steffie and don't look at her again for the rest of the period.

"Heather?"

I consider not answering Matt's knock at the door of Dove Cottage except he sounds worried.

"Heather? I need your help."

"What?" It's only four-thirty but it's been raining off and on all afternoon and the clouds make it seem like it's already starting to get dark.

"You have to help me with a costume."

"Costume?" I open the door and let him come inside.

"For Halloween." Matt shifts from foot to foot.

"It's only October fourth! Halloween's nearly a month away! Talk to Mom."

I turn back to my notebook. Describing dead bodies is harder than I thought. They get stiff after a while so it's hard for Charlene to turn the corpse over by herself but she doesn't want to ask for help because she's afraid she'll be accused of the murder.

I write several more sentences describing the hay chute in the loft floor (Charlene finds the body in a folded-up position in one of the hay mangers which makes it really hard to even get a look at the murder victim's face) when I realize Matt is still standing in the doorway.

"What's wrong now? Mom always helps you with your costume. If you must start getting ready so early, ask her."

Matt picks up the big seashell I have sitting on my windowsill and turns it over in his hands.

"Mom's . . . busy."

Busy. That's an interesting way of putting it. Busy napping. Since Mom got back from Ontario she's been slowing down like a music box that needs to be wound. At first, she tried to get back into her regular routine at the clinic, but it seemed like just keeping up made her incredibly tired. We're still seeing a lot of Dr. deBoer—and his wife who keeps bringing the baby by. Poor Brian hasn't had much time off since Mom came back from Ontario.

Twice this week Mom didn't even come out of the bedroom in the morning to help us get ready. Dad was the one who made sure I had a lunch and got out the door early enough to catch the school bus. Matt has started heading over to Alyssum's house with whatever books he needs without even waiting for Mom to tell him. She hasn't had the energy to see her usual number of patients and halfway through the day, she needs a nap. A couple of times she has slept right through dinner. She goes to bed even earlier than Matt!

Dad says she's recovering from all the stress of her trip and the funeral.

"Did you ask her to help you?" I ask Matt. My brother's favourite holiday of the whole year, outside of Christmas, is Halloween. Making a costume with Mom is an annual tradition.

He nods. "She said she was too far behind with her work. She said to ask you."

Ask me? What about my work? I'm still behind at

school and I haven't figured out how to get the body out of the hay manger. Matt sighs and bites his bottom lip. Sometimes he looks so pathetic.

"What do you want to be? A ghost?" A ghost would be easy to make—a sheet with a couple of holes cut out for eyes . . .

"Pepper."

"What?"

"It's Alyssum's idea. Mrs. Cranwell told us about the Halloween bonfire and Kid-Fest at the Community Centre and then Alyssum said we could be salt and pepper shakers and I didn't have a better idea so I guess I'm pepper."

"A pepper shaker? That's going to be hard to make."

Matt shoots me a triumphant glare.

"Exactly why I have to start working on my costume now."

"We can ask Dad. . . ."

Even as I say it I know that's not practical. Dad really is busy. Not only is he doing more and more of the chores around the farm, clinic, and kennels, he's also working on a big commission—two large paintings which are supposed to be ready by Christmas for a couple who live in Vancouver.

"How can you even go trick-or-treating here?" There are no suburbs on Tarragon Island. The houses are far apart and half of them are completely hidden at the end of very long driveways. It seems totally impractical to go from door to door.

"Alyssum said that there's a trick-or-treat party at the Community Centre. People bring candy and set stuff up on card tables. You get to go from table to table for treats."

"That seems like cheating to me."

Matt pushes his bottom lip out. "It's not that easy. Alyssum says they make you sing or tell a joke at each table before you get anything. There's a costume parade and prizes and a big bonfire. . . ."

It's obvious Matt is determined to participate in the island festivities.

"I'll phone Alyssum after dinner," I offer. "Maybe she has a plan for how to make the costumes. It was her idea."

"Okay," he says, and darts away into the gathering darkness.

I shudder. The cool autumn air is making it chilly to work out in Dove Cottage, especially after dark. I gather my notebooks and pens and follow my younger brother into the house.

"Kids—I have something to tell you."

Dad globs a disintegrating square of lasagna onto my plate. Matt and I look at Mom's empty chair and then back at each other. It's not the first time since she came back that she's opted for a nap instead of dinner. My stomach clutches and I put down my fork, my appetite suddenly gone. This is it, I figure—Dad's going to tell us how Mom has leukemia and she's tired all the time because she's dying and then Matt and I will have to be brave and help him as much as we can. . . .

"Granny is coming to stay with us for a while."

Matt looks up like a startled rabbit. My breath hisses out between my lips and I realize I had temporarily stopped breathing.

My first thought is that it will be good to see Granny again. My second is that it will be awful to have both Granny and Mom moping around. And then my next thought is that I don't want to move out of my bedroom. I'm just getting used to it!

"Where will she sleep?"

Dad launches into what seems to be a well-rehearsed speech.

"Your grandmother will arrive on Saturday. That gives us all week to clear out the stuff from the dining room."

"She's going to sleep in here?" Matt looks appalled. "There's no room for a bed!"

"There will be if we move the dining room table out to the barn."

"We're going to eat in the barn?"

I kick Matt under the table.

"No. In the kitchen. We'll put the extra leaf in the table. That will give us enough room."

"Why?" I ask. "Why is she coming? Who's going to look after the farm in Guelph?"

"Your grandmother is finding it very hard to stay on the farm alone. She says she needs to get away for a while. She has organized a team of neighbours to help watch things. Mrs. Pratchet's son and daughter-in-law are going to live in her house while she's here. And, she misses you and wants to give your mother a hand."

A stab of anger lodges right below my ribcage. Everybody is helping Mom already. Dad has practically taken over the entire household, Matt and I are doing extra chores, Brian may as well be running the clinic on his own, and Alyssum and her family have totally taken over Mom's teaching responsibilities. She isn't even doing her twice-weekly science lessons with Matt and Alyssum like she promised.

What about the rest of us? That's what I want to know. Shouldn't Mom be looking after us?

We finish the rest of our meal in silence. When Matt asks if we can go over to the Cranwells' after dinner, Dad gives us a distracted nod. It seems to me we could ask him for anything and he'd go along with it.

"Be back by eight," is all he says. "Heather, you can help me move all the furniture out of here tomorrow after school."

It's only later, when we are walking down our driveway following the wedge of light from our flash-light beam, that the questions begin to flood my brain. How long will Granny be staying? Will she help shop and make the meals or will we have to look after her, too? If Mom is still so upset about Grandpa's death, then how distraught will Granny be?

It's always a bit of a surprise to come upon the Cranwells' house, especially after dark. They live in an underground home, and when you come down the driveway, all you can see is a mound of grass with a chimney sticking out of it. At night, warm yellow light glows upwards from skylights sunk partially into the ground. To get in, we have to follow a path around the edge of the hump that hides the house. The path leads to a patio area and the front door.

When the door swings open and Mrs. Cranwell greets us, the first thing I notice is how warm it is inside. Then I'm overwhelmed by the doughy scent of baking bread.

Chapter Seven

Collected Quote #94
'Twixt the optimist and pessimist
The difference is droll:
The optimist sees the doughnut
But the pessimist sees the hole.—McLandburgh Wilson

Like most of her projects, Alyssum's plan for the salt and pepper costumes is elaborate.

"After we make the chicken wire frames we'll layer over everything with papier mâché."

"How will we get inside?"

"We'll make the costumes in two halves," she explains. "Mom can fasten them together once we've stepped inside. Look. I did a sketch."

Alyssum rifles through a messy stack of magazines, newspapers, and bits and pieces of paper on her work table. "Here."

We all lean over the drawing.

"That doesn't look like salt and pepper shakers. They look like two fire hydrants. What are these things?" I point at two orange blobs on the front of the costumes.

"UNICEF boxes. Halloween is one of my best fundraisers." She says it like she invented the collection process.

"They look like name tags," Matt says.

"Fine. You do better."

Matt takes a pencil and begins to draw on the back of Alyssum's picture. He draws slowly and deliberately, stopping every so often to close his eyes. I guess he must see the picture in his head because when he opens his eyes again and continues, he adds something that actually makes his picture look more like the object. In his sketch, the UNICEF boxes look three-dimensional. He even adds coin slots. Of the two of us, Matt is definitely the one who inherited the drawing gene.

"That's pretty good," Alyssum says.

Matt shrugs. "How will we make the caps?"

"Tinfoil over cardboard. We'll poke three holes for pepper and eight for salt. We can paint the rest of the shakers and add a big *S* and a *P* so nobody thinks we're—"

"Fire hydrants," Matt finishes for her.

Mrs. Cranwell taps at Alyssum's bedroom door and pushes her way in with a platter laden with slabs of buttered bread and a pot of homemade jam. Just the smell makes my mouth water.

"How are you making out?"

"Our costumes will be so great! We're making these wire frames—see how Matt drew them! And then we'll paint and . . ."

"When's Halloween?" Mrs. Cranwell grins. "You'd better get started."

Alyssum nods vigorously. Matt looks pained.

"I . . . uhhh . . . I don't know how much time we'll have at home," I say. "I mean, my grandmother is coming to stay and my mom is still . . . um . . . getting caught up at the clinic. . . ."

The look on Matt's face changes from worry to gratitude. I guess he's glad I said something about all the strangeness at home. It saves him having to explain, though I suspect Mrs. Cranwell already knows more than she's letting on.

Mrs. Cranwell holds up her hand. "Not to worry. You two can make the costumes as part of this month's art project."

Matt manages a small smile. "That's great," he says.

"What are you going to be, Heather?"

"Ummm . . . I hadn't really—I mean, I wasn't going to . . ."

"You have to dress up!" Alyssum exclaims. "You could be oil . . . or vinegar!"

We all laugh.

"Leave her alone, Alyssum. I'm sure Heather will come up with something. There's a Halloween dance at the high school, isn't there?"

"I heard something like that. . . ." I've never been to a dance before and see no reason to start now.

Alyssum's eyes sparkle with fun. "Have you got a date yet?"

Matt looks at me like I've grown horns.

"I'm not planning on going."

"Oh!" Alyssum says like she just remembered something important. "Did you . . ." She looks at her mother and then back at me. "Did you say you were doing a socials project about Russia? I have a good book you can borrow."

Russia? We aren't studying Russia. I have no clue what Alyssum's going on about. We're studying life in Ancient Rome.

"It has information in it about the economy, geography, the Russian flag . . . STAMPS . . . all kinds of stuff."

"Oh—great. Yes, that would be good to borrow."

When the door closes behind Alyssum's mother, Matt leans forward.

"What was that all about? You're studying Russia?"

"No," Alyssum says.

"You nearly blew it," I say.

"I couldn't help it—when we were talking about the high school it just popped into my head!"

"What's going on?" Matt asks.

"Can we trust him?" Alyssum asks me.

I can't see what harm it would do to tell him. All this secrecy doesn't make sense to me anyway. "Sure," I say with a shrug.

Alyssum fills Matt in on the strange stamps and Matt's eyes light up.

"They were stolen!" he exclaims.

"What! Stolen?" Alyssum looks horrified.

"How would you know that?" I ask, convinced he's making up a story to get attention.

Matt is beside himself with excitement. "I read about it in the *Tarragon Times*."

"*You* read about it?" Matt pushes his lips together and looks hurt. I wish I hadn't said anything. When he gets that look, he can be stubborn. It's just that Matt's dyslexic and doesn't read anything if he doesn't absolutely have to.

"What did the article say?" Alyssum bounces up and down on her toes. "Tell us!"

"Not much. It was one of the shortest articles in the paper. But I had to pick something for our current events project."

Alyssum's face splits into a huge, happy grin. "I found some very cool stuff for my project on the *New York Times* website—but they didn't say anything about stolen stamps on Tarragon Island."

"Duh—I guess not." I grab Alyssum's shoulders. "Would you stop bouncing? You're making me seasick."

"Not" (bounce) "until" (bounce bounce) "I hear" (bounce bounce) "what Matt knows."

"The article just said that a local resident reported several thousand dollars worth of stamps missing from her elderly father's collection."

"That's it? No names?"

Alyssum stops bouncing and flops onto her bed. "I wonder if that's confidential information?"

I shrug. "Can people look at police reports? I mean, if we went down to the police station and asked, would they let us see the file?"

Matt and Alyssum stare back at me blankly. We are hardly candidates for running a successful detective agency. We don't know a thing about how crimes are investigated. I wish now I had taken Eric's advice and ordered that book.

"In the movies the detectives always have sources—you know, people who work in the office who can secretly photocopy information," I say.

"Do you know anyone who works for the RCMP?" Matt asks Alyssum hopefully. Alyssum has lived on Tarragon Island her whole life and knows pretty well everybody.

"Constable Rosen buys eggs from us. But I don't know how to ask without seeming very suspicious."

"What if we just phone the RCMP office and ask? Maybe we wouldn't have to give our names," Matt says.

It seems so obvious I'm convinced it won't work, but Alyssum wastes no time in running out of the room to get the phone. She dials the number for the police station and the phone rings and rings. Finally, she hangs up.

"Nobody there. The answering machine said to leave a name and number."

"Nobody there? What if we were being robbed right now?" Matt looks more than a little disturbed.

"You wouldn't call the office number, you'd call 911."

"Why don't we call 911, then?"

"You can't do that unless it's an emergency," Alyssum says firmly.

"True. I think you can go to jail if you call 911 without having a good reason," I say.

"Now what?" Matt asks.

Alyssum sinks back against the pillow. "I guess I could try calling the police station tomorrow during the day," Alyssum says. "Maybe someone will be in the office then."

"Wait a minute now," I say. "What are we trying to find out exactly?"

"Who owns the stamps. Maybe there's a reward."

"What if the owners are responsible?"

Matt and Alyssum stare at me like I've lost my mind.

"You know, insurance fraud or something. Maybe the owners are pretending the stamps were stolen so they can get the insurance money."

"I didn't think of that. There must be a way to find out who it is," Alyssum insists. "Everybody knows everybody on this island. Surely someone will know who was robbed."

"Why don't you just hand the stamps over to the police and let them deal with it?"

"Because it might be a mistake. I don't want to get anyone in trouble. We can figure it out."

I shake my head. Alyssum is like a terrier with a stolen slipper when she latches on to an idea.

"Don't look at me like that," she says. "How about we investigate for two weeks and if we haven't solved the mystery by then we'll hand the stamps over?"

"How's it going in there?"

We all jump as if we've been caught committing a crime.

"Fine!" Alyssum says quickly as her mother comes into the room.

"I'm sorry to interrupt, but it's nearly eight and I think Heather has an early start tomorrow to catch the bus?"

Though Alyssum's mother phrases her comment like a question, I can tell she's dropping a pretty broad hint that we shouldn't stay too much longer.

"What time will you be here tomorrow, Matt?"

Matt mumbles something about chores and finishing building a nesting box for two of his cockatiels, Ferdinand and Dolce.

"Shall we say nine-thirty?"

"I guess."

If Matt could, he'd sleep until noon every day and later on the weekends. I think he hoped home-schooling would be easier than going to the Tarragon Island Elementary School. It hasn't worked out that way. Like Matt says, you can't hide in the back row at Alyssum's kitchen table.

Chapter Eight

Collected Quote #97
She'll wish there was more, and that's the great art o'
letter-writin'.—Charles Dickens

Dear Maggie:
   I am turning into a horrible person. It's not my fault—I
mean, inside I'm still the same old me (don't worry, I'm
still your friend, your best friend).

   I roll my fountain pen back and forth between my
palms. How can I say I'm still Maggie's best friend?
She lives practically at the other end of the country.
Who knows when I'll ever see her again?

   She certainly used to be my best friend. When we
lived in Toronto, Maggie and I used to walk to school
together every morning. Sometimes we'd stop at
McCormick's Confectionery and buy penny candy.

   My favourites were the little peppermint balls. I
could get six for a quarter. Maggie always bought one
of those stretchy candy bracelets. She could make one
bracelet last a whole week! Not me—give me candy
and I just keep eating until it's all gone.

   That's how it is when you know someone really
well. You know everything about them—like how
Maggie often wears two different-coloured socks. I
don't mean two different shades of grey-used-to-be-
white gym socks, I mean one yellow sock and one red
sock. She likes ice tea with lemon and collects
postcards of fish. She likes stationery stores almost as

much as I do but she prefers soaking in the bathtub (I like fast showers).

I still know all those things about her and I don't know anyone here on Tarragon Island nearly that well (except my family and I don't think a person can be best friends with their relatives, at least, not the ones you live with). So, that must mean she's still my best friend by default. Unless she's changed the way I've changed and then I wouldn't like her any more.

The unfinished letter in front of me is about the tenth attempt I've made to write. At first I started writing all about Grandpa dying and how Mom is still so upset and how sometimes in the middle of doing something totally different I think about Grandpa and start crying. That letter was so sad I threw it out. Who would want to read something so miserable?

Then I wrote a cheerful letter about how my writing was going and how I'm starting work on my mystery novel and it just sounded false, like I was trying to sound happy but was really languishing in the black depths of despair. After that I tried to write really honestly about school and how much I can't stand Steffie and all the other cool girls and it sounded whiny and I realized that I wasn't really writing honestly anyway since I had neglected to mention how I was just as bad as those girls because of what I said about Eric.

What finally gets me writing again is the thought that if Maggie had changed for the worst I would want to know about it or I would feel tricked into staying her best friend. Like it or not, Maggie is going to find out how awful I really am.

There's this boy, Eric, in Grade 8. He's fourteen but he's really scrawny—you, know, like Shawn Hennessey? I know him from my writing group at the Community Centre. He's a really good writer—he's the one who made me think I should try writing a mystery.

I decide not to explain how that all happened sort of by accident. Writing down the absolute truth is very hard because when you look at things from one side, everything seems very clear, but when you turn things around or focus on different details, the "truth" suddenly changes.

Anyway, Eric is like a total skateboard freak. He even tries to ride down the halls at school, even though the principal, Mrs. Gurney, keeps confiscating his board. He's got all these skateboarding friends who wear elbow pads to class and they're always joking around and wearing weird hats to disguise their helmets. At first, they seem kind of scary, but I think they're just trying to make an impression.

It turns out that Eric is one of the only people at school who has ever spontaneously said anything nice to me. Well, Steffie and Co. talk to me but I think that's mostly because they feel obliged. Steffie was assigned to be my buddy on the first day of school so she pretty well has to speak to me. The other cool girls follow her lead. Since it was easy to hang out with her, I've kind of fallen into the habit of just talking to this one little group, you know? And the other kids are all in their groups and I can't just barge in and say, "Hey, I want to be your friend."

I put my pen down and rub my hands together, trying to get the blood flowing into my chilled fingers. I pull the cuffs of my thick sweater down until my hands mostly disappear, clutch my pen in my half-numb hand, and continue with the letter.

So, we were all sitting outside smoking . . .

I wasn't actually smoking, but passed the cigarette

from Alicia on one side of me to Terri on the other. If Maggie was going to see me as bad, she might as well have plenty of reason.

...when everyone started talking about the Halloween Dance. Everybody was going with some boy or other and then Steffie asked me, "Who do you like?" and I had to say something so I said, "Eric."

I don't know why I said his name—he's not even in my grade and I hardly know him and I doubt he's even going to the dance and if he does go he'll probably go with his whole skateboarding gang.

But I did say his name and then they all laughed and right then, who came rolling past? Yup. Eric and his friends.

Before I could try to stop her, Steffie yelled out, "Hey, loverboy! What are you wearing to the dance?"

He spun his board around, stepped on one end so it stood straight up, and then grabbed the other end. His friends all whistled and hooted like this was the coolest thing anyone could do with a skateboard and then Eric said, "Who wants to know?" and he looked right at me!

And then, I don't know why, I said to Steffie, "I didn't mean Eric—I got his name confused with someone else. I wouldn't go to a dance with a freak like him!"

The candle flickers as a draft catches the flame. I swallow hard as I remember the look on Eric's face—first his cocky grin, then the hurt when his eyes met mine for just a second, and then the flush of disgust and anger as he turned his back on us, dropped his board to the ground, and pushed off.

The other girls laughed hysterically.

"I didn't think you could mean a total loser like that!"

I felt like crying or running after Eric to apologize or telling Steffie and Co. to shut up but I didn't do anything like that. What I did makes me feel sick, like

I want to cut out a rotten part of myself. I tipped my head back and laughed louder than any of them.

I explain all this as well as I can in the letter and fold the paper into an envelope. I seal it up before I can change my mind. I don't want to tell Maggie, but I know it's the right thing to do and maybe, if I do this one right thing, it will help balance out the wrong thing I did to Eric.

"Heather!" Dad's voice is sharp. I won't look at him and the fact I'm staring into my creamy pea soup like it's the most interesting thing I've ever encountered in my life is making him madder and madder.

"Heather—you will apologize to your mother."

Nobody at the kitchen table moves. Mom has joined us for a change, though she hasn't said anything for hours. That's what caused the whole problem in the first place.

Ever since Granny arrived on Saturday she hasn't stopped working. She brought special German sausage all the way from Guelph in her carry-on baggage just so she could whip up Mom's favourite breakfast on Sunday.

Mom has slowed down so much it seems like any time now she's going to stall out and fall off the edge of her own little planet. Granny seems to have sped up so much she's doing the work of a small army.

It's Granny's fourth day here and she's already scrubbed the crusty pancake dribbles from the front of the stove, taken apart all the light fixtures and washed out the dead flies, and scraped that green and black stuff out of the bottom of the vegetable crisper.

Yesterday was Thanksgiving and she recruited Matt to help her prepare the meal. Between the two of them they produced the most amazing Thanksgiving dinner any of us have ever tasted.

Tonight we're having leftovers plus Granny's specialty, homemade pea soup with chunks of ham. The reason Dad's so mad he could spit tacks is because I said something stupid when Granny asked me to pass Mom the dinner buns.

That was the last straw. There's Mom sitting like a lump on her chair, staring down at her hands in her lap, not looking up, not saying anything, not saying thank you, not offering to help, not doing anything and I said, "I'll pass the rolls when Mom says, 'Please.'"

I figured it was time someone made a point—I mean, Matt and I are supposed to be polite so I think the least Mom can do is say please and thank you.

Dad, for one, doesn't seem to agree. I can feel his glare burning holes in the top of my head.

"Look at me when I'm talking to you."

He's really furious now and I wait for Mom to intervene on my behalf, to say, "It's okay, Ben. Heather's right—I should say 'please pass the buns' . . ." but she stays totally silent.

Beside me, Matt starts to quiver and I can tell he's trying not to burst out laughing and to my horror, the minute I realize what he's doing, I feel a bubble of laughter welling up inside me.

I try really hard to think of something hideous and disgusting but nothing comes to me quickly enough to save me and I can't stop the burble of a half-stifled giggle from escaping.

"That's enough!" Dad's voice is so loud both Matt and I jump and then we both lose control and start giggling.

"Both of you—to your rooms!"

We waste no time fleeing from the table. The minute we're in the upstairs hall all desire to laugh has completely gone.

"Why'd you have to talk back?" Matt says. "I'm hungry."

"Why'd you have to go and laugh? If you hadn't done that we'd still be in there."

"Maybe. You should leave Mom alone. I think she's sick or something."

I don't want to admit this might be true.

"No, she's not. She's just acting like a big baby. She should grow up."

My own words shock me. Matt says, "Maybe you should grow up yourself, Heather." Then he disappears into his bedroom and closes the door behind him very quietly.

I stick my tongue out at his door and then in the general direction of the grown-ups downstairs and stalk into my room. I slam my bedroom door as hard as I can, satisfied to note that the bang rattles the glass in my window.

Chapter Nine

Collected Quote #18
Writing for me was always an inside thing. It's always been the way in which I maintain my sanity.—William Gibson

I don't like being in a bad mood at school, but after the big dinner blow-out last night my mood has gone from bad to positively evil. In fact, I don't remember ever feeling worse.

Everything anybody says irritates me. This morning when Granny asked if I wanted raisins in my oatmeal I said, "I don't like oatmeal." I didn't even try to say it nicely. Granny sighed and carefully put the pan back on the stove.

I wanted to apologize, but I didn't know what for since I was just being honest. I grabbed a muffin to eat on the school bus and left the house even earlier than usual.

Dad was already out in the studio, painting, and Mom and Matt were still in bed. Poor Granny was still standing by the stove when I left the house.

The old woman raised her hand to her forehead and Writer Girl saw how tired she looked. The old woman's glasses rested on her chest, suspended on a string of tiny white pearls. They rose and fell with each breath she took, changing the angle of the lenses just enough to reflect the light in a series of slow winks.

Ever since I got to school I've been making these

notes in the margins of my notebooks, all of which have something to do with why my teachers and the other kids in my class are dumb, ugly, or uncoordinated. It doesn't matter who I observe, every single person I watch is nasty and disgusting in some way. I thought making notes would help me forget about how I left Granny. I want to believe she moved away from the stove, but I keep seeing her there, stuck exactly where I left her.

To distract myself I write about Mr. McGuire, my math teacher.

Pointy beak nose, skull-like cheekbones, pasty skin— doesn't know how to shave (razor nick above and to the right of his poky-out Adam's apple). Boring, dull, stupid— doesn't know what he's talking about. Should have been a mortician, not someone who teaches kids.

I wish I could say my observations somehow make me feel better, but that's not true. I feel worse and worse as the day wears on.

At lunch I run into the bathroom by the office because I know Steffie and Co. always use the other one by the science room. I hide in a stall and give them lots of time to primp and preen and go outside. When I come out into the hallway I stop dead in my tracks. A tall, elegant woman wearing a long, black coat is putting something beside the stamp-collection box. She swoops past me, humming softly to herself, her long coat billowing out behind her. When she's gone I check to see what kind of contribution she's made.

My heart thuds when I see she has left a Tamolinos box on the table. I spin around and run out to the parking lot but the woman has completely disappeared.

Still moving fast, I fly into the office to ask Mr. Bell who the woman was.

"Where's Mr. Bell?" I ask Mrs. Franklin, the school librarian, who is the only one behind the desk in the office.

"He only works here part-time," she says. "He's at his other job today. When he's not here the teachers take turns staffing the office."

"Oh. Well, did you happen to notice that woman?"

"What woman? Nobody's come in here in the last little while."

"No—she didn't come in here. She dropped some stamps off. I was just wondering who . . ." It's obvious Mrs. Franklin was paying no attention to traffic out in the hall.

"Never mind," I say, and back out of the office.

At the table, I can't resist. I lift the lid of the Tamolinos box and look inside. The box is filled with a jumble of stamps. Most are Canadian and many of them are still stuck on corners of envelopes. They don't look very valuable, not like the neatly organized set of Russian stamps Alyssum showed us. Those had been lined up neatly on special collecting pages and little notes had been written in pencil beside each one.

"Could I please use the phone?"

Mrs. Franklin looks a little annoyed to be bothered again. She's trying to type something on the computer.

"On the counter. Don't be long."

"Alyssum? It's me, Heather. I'm phoning from school."

I glance over at Mrs. Franklin who is typing away as fast as she can. She's paying no attention whatso-ever to me.

"There's another Tamolinos box here. Should I bring it home with me?"

There's a squeal of excitement and then a pause at the other end of the phone line. I study the back of

Mrs. Franklin's head while I wait for Alyssum to come back on the line again.

"It's okay," Alyssum says. I can practically see her bouncing up and down with excitement. "My mom's going to town a little later. I'll get her to pick up the box. Did you see who dropped it off?"

"Yup," I say. "A woman in a long, black coat."

"But who was it? What's her name? Didn't anybody else see her?"

"I don't know, I have no idea, and apparently not."

Alyssum makes an exasperated little sound and says, "Well, try to find out, okay? That's probably the thief!"

I want to ask why on earth the thief keeps giving away the stolen goods but I don't want to risk being overheard.

"Fine. I'll see you later."

I walk out of the office and a thought suddenly hits me. If the Russian stamps really were stolen, then Alyssum is in possession of stolen property. If that's the case, she could be in a lot of trouble if she doesn't go to the police.

I don't think they're likely to arrest a ten-year-old kid, but maybe they would fine her parents or something since it's probably not helping their investigation that Alyssum is hanging on to the evidence.

The rest of the afternoon drags on and on. All I can think about is getting home, avoiding my whole family, and going straight over to Alyssum's to talk some sense into her. She has to turn in the stamps or we could both be in a lot of trouble.

"But, Dad! I have to go to Alyssum's house. I need to talk to her about . . . school. A school assignment . . ." I look over towards the closed dining room door with a pang of guilt. I wonder if Granny said anything to Dad about this morning. I'm not sure if she's in there or not, but I lower my voice anyway.

I know Dad knows I'm lying. It doesn't make sense that Alyssum would be helping me. Dad starts to speak but I jump in and say, "She needs some information. . . ."

Dad looks up when Mia trots into the kitchen. Mia's dog tags clink against the rim of her empty water bowl. She stares at the bowl, panting, and then looks up at Dad.

"Empty. Again." He levels an accusing look in my direction.

"It's not my job."

"Heather. How old are you?"

He knows very well how old I am. My thirteenth birthday wasn't that long ago.

"You're old enough to be able to see when a job needs doing." Water sloshes onto the floor when he fills Mia's bowl and puts it on the floor. "Old enough that I shouldn't have to ask you to take the food scraps to the compost pile or lend a hand with the dishes."

"I help!"

He sighs. "You're not listening. Yes, you do help, but only after I've asked and sometimes several times. Your help isn't worth having if I have to ask for it."

I feel like saying, "If it's not worth having, don't take it," but I restrain myself and study the tablecloth. It's dirty where Matt sits. He must have dribbled some spaghetti sauce.

Mia finishes her drink and trots back out of the kitchen. It's pretty convenient how she came in right when Dad was about to give me a lecture.

"Am I done?"

"No. That wasn't what I wanted to talk to you about."

The way his brown eyes stare straight into mine sends a shudder right through me. The lines at the corner of his left eye twitch so the skin on his cheek stretches and lifts.

"Your mother is at the hospital."

"Why?"

"She wouldn't . . . well, she couldn't get up this morning."

"What do you mean? What's wrong with her?"

My heart races, bashes at the inside of my chest.

"Heather, your mother hasn't been herself since Grandpa died."

As if I hadn't noticed. What did that have to do with being at the hospital?

"Everyone feels sad when someone special dies. That's quite normal." Dad's voice sounds very calm, like he's been practising. "But sometimes that sadness gets so deep, so strong, that it overwhelms a person. That's what happened to your mother. The doctor says she's depressed."

"Depressed? We're all depressed about Grandpa dying and we're not in the hospital."

"Well, no. We're all sad about it, but that's not the same thing as being clinically depressed. Granny is there with her now."

"Why isn't Granny depressed? Grandpa was her husband."

"Heather, please try to understand."

Outside, Matt thumps up the steps and slams through the back door.

"Dad?"

He runs down the back hall, Mia's nails clattering on the floor behind him.

"Hi, Matt. I put the lasagna in about half an hour ago, just like you said."

Matt grins. "Okay—we can do the garlic bread at about 5:45. Dinner at six? Will Mom eat with us?"

"She's at the . . ."

Dad talks right over me, silencing me with his stare. "She's out having coffee with your grandmother. I'm on my way out to pick them up. I don't know if they will have eaten already."

I'm not sure why Dad hasn't said anything to Matt about where Mom really is, but I hold my tongue and wait to see what's coming next.

"How's your costume coming?" Dad asks, neatly changing the subject.

"Great! Alyssum and I worked on the mesh frames today. Except for the tops. We're going to make those out of cardboard because we don't want to get stabbed in the head by chicken wire."

I try to listen to Matt babble on and on about his Halloween costume, but I can't get Mom out of my mind. Images of Mom lying semi-comatose in her darkened room with her eyes half-closed push into my mind along with a whole lot of questions. If she's at the hospital, how come Dad's picking her up in time for dinner? Why does someone who's sad have to go to the hospital in the first place?

"Heather? Are you ready to go? They should be ready by now."

"Can I come?" Matt asks.

Dad shakes his head and cuffs Matt lightly on the shoulder.

"Sorry, little man. I need to discuss Heather's recent rude behaviour in private."

Matt tries to suppress a smirk but doesn't quite manage. I grab a cookie from the jar and sink my teeth into its soft, chewy sweetness.

"We're almost out of cookies," I mumble through my mouthful of chocolate chips.

"I'll start another batch while you're out."

I know Matt offers to bake because he feels sorry for me that I'm getting into trouble. That makes me feel a little guilty since I know I'm not really getting in trouble but Dad wants me to come along so we can finish our conversation about Mom.

In the car Dad says, "I didn't want to upset Matt. He's too young to understand. It's better if he just thinks Mom is still sad because of Grandpa. Your mother will be fine. It's not necessary to worry him."

"But why did she have to go to the hospital?"

"To see the psychiatrist. He only comes to the island once a month. Your mom was lucky to get in to see him. There was a cancellation . . . and, depression can be serious."

"A shrink? Mom's sad, not crazy!"

"She's not crazy, Heather. Depression is a kind of mental illness—a sickness of the brain just like a cold is a sickness of the body."

The trees blur into a wave of greeny grey outside the car window. Mom mentally ill? What did that mean? Didn't people like that get locked up in mental hospitals with bars on the windows? Or wind up pushing shopping carts loaded with blankets and shoes around downtown?

"What's the shrink doing to her?"

"He's not doing anything to her. He was going to talk to her and then she'll probably be given some pills to take for a while—just until . . ."

"Pills?" The word catches in my throat almost like I tried to swallow an aspirin without any water.

"Heather, it's okay. Don't cry."

"Mom's not crazy!" I sob. "I'll help more! She's just tired, that's all. She's not a nutcase!" My nails press into the palms of my clenched fists.

Gravel crunches under the car tires as Dad pulls over to the side of the road. I bury my face in his scratchy sweater and feel his arms around me.

"Shhhh, Heather. Your mother will be fine."

"The . . . the . . . pills," I sob. "How long does she have to . . ."

"It's hard to say. Six months? A year? Maybe longer."

"Ohhhh noooo . . ." I can hardly breathe I'm crying so hard.

"What, Heather? The pills will help her. She'll be able to eat again, and her energy will come back and soon she'll be back to her old self!"

"She's going to be a drug addict!" In my mind I can see it clearly—my mother lying in bed begging for her medication, her hand shaking as she reaches for her pill.

I collapse against my father's chest. "No . . . no . . . no . . ."

"Heather! Stop it! You're overreacting!"

"No I'm not! My mother is crazy! She's going to be a drug addict and . . . and . . ."

"Stop it right now."

Telling someone to stop sobbing is not the way to stop someone from crying. To prove this I cry harder.

"I can't . . ." I gasp.

"Listen to me. Lots of people get depressed. The medication your mom has to take for a while is not the kind of thing that's addictive. It will help her brain chemicals get back to normal so she can get back to normal so our lives can get back to normal."

I shudder. What if I can't stop crying? Would that

mean I'm depressed, too? Maybe this is all a trick? Maybe Dad thinks I'm crazy and he's taking me to the hospital to the psychiatrist and they'll give me drugs and turn me into a zombie.

That works. I stifle my sniffles and sit up. Dad hands me a tissue.

"I'm fine," I snuffle.

"I know this is a shock, Heather. It's all a little scary. Until a few days ago I didn't know any more about depression than you do."

He pulls the car back onto the road and continues into town.

"There's a library book at home you can look at. It should answer a lot of your questions. For now, I'm not going to say anything to Matt. He's too young to understand."

I nod, though I'm not sure I agree. Matt's smart. He knows something's going on. He was the one who guessed Mom is sick.

Mom and Granny are waiting for us just inside the hospital doors. I study them as they walk towards the car, searching for signs that Mom's talk with the shrink might have knocked some sense into her, made her see how hard it has been to live with her recently.

I get out of the car so Mom can sit in the front. I'm almost exactly the same height as my mother and we are both nearly a head taller than Granny. We're all a bit on the round side, though Mom is the roundest. Then again . . . when she draws her jacket around her I see how much weight she's lost over the past few weeks. It's especially obvious when she pauses for a second with her hand on the car door and I look right into her face.

Her cheeks are usually plump and full, with a

dimple in each. But now, her cheeks are beginning to hollow and she looks very pale. Her dark hair falls forward and for a second we meet each other's eyes. But her eyes are different, almost like she doesn't recognize me.

I scuttle over in the back seat and make room for Granny beside me.

Writer Girl's mother sighs heavily and buckles her seatbelt without saying a word. She leans her head back against the headrest and closes her eyes. Writer Girl stares straight ahead, acutely aware of the slight wheeziness of her grandmother's breathing.

"Everything okay?" Dad asks Mom, who gives a small nod in reply.

"Matt stayed home to bake," he says from the front seat as we drive away from the hospital. "I told Heather what's going on."

Mom doesn't say anything at first. Her head bumps from side to side as we turn onto the road. "Mmm," she says, finally.

It's then I understand. It's not that she doesn't recognize me—that's not why she seems to tune everything out. With a sick, desperate sort of feeling deep in my middle I realize she just doesn't care any more. Knowing that makes me more scared than I've ever been in my whole life.

The old woman in the back seat reaches over and covers Writer Girl's hand with hers. Writer Girl concentrates on the back of her father's headrest and counts the stitches that run around its perimeter. She does not pull her hand away. In fact, when the old woman squeezes her lightly, Writer Girl turns and gives her a little smile.

Chapter Ten

Collected Quote #75
I blame myself for not often enough seeing the extraordinary in the ordinary. Somewhere in his journals Dostoyevsky remarks that a writer can begin anywhere, at the most commonplace thing, scratch around in it long enough, pray and dig away long enough, and lo!, soon he will hit upon the marvelous.—Saul Bellow

"Alyssum called twice while you were out."

Matt's in the kitchen blobbing the last dollops of cookie dough onto a pan when we walk in.

"Smells good!" Dad says, rubbing his stomach.

"I just took the lasagna out of the oven," Matt says, waving the spatula at the dish filled nearly to overflowing with warm, bubbling cheese, pasta, and meat sauce.

"I'll stick these cookies in so we have dessert and then we can eat. Five minutes . . ."

He doesn't ask Mom if she wants to eat and she doesn't say anything as she shrugs out of her coat, pads down the hallway, and disappears into the bedroom.

"I've got time to quickly call Alyssum," I say, wanting to draw attention away from Mom. Matt is curious about why Alyssum called, I can tell, but he doesn't say anything since Dad's in the room.

"Are you hungry, Granny?"

"Absolutely, my darling chef. My mouth is watering already!"

I dial quickly.

"Hi, Alyssum."

"Heather! What took you so long? I picked up the box this afternoon—"

"And??"

"And nothing. They're just old junk stamps like I'm used to getting. Nothing even half valuable."

"Oh." I don't know what I'd hoped for, but certainly more than what she was telling me.

"Did you find out about the woman in black?"

"No."

Dad is still in the kitchen, setting the table, so I have to be careful not to give anything away.

"Can you come over?" Alyssum asks.

"Um . . . no . . ."

Granny is sitting at the kitchen table pantomiming how great dinner looks by rubbing her tummy, licking her lips, and rolling her eyes towards the ceiling.

"Why not?" Alyssum is insistent. "I have big news!"

"Just tell me quickly."

"Why can't you come over?"

"I just can't." I can't even explain why. It's like I suddenly feel totally exhausted and just want to sit down, or go to bed.

"The police came to our house today."

"What!" That perks me up. I can't ask any pointed questions since there are too many listening ears around.

"They asked me if I had seen any Russian stamps when I was at the stamp shop in Victoria. They know I go over there a lot to sell my stamps."

"What did you say?"

"No. I said, 'No, I've never seen Russian stamps in Victoria.'"

"You didn't tell them?" I can't believe what I'm hearing.

"Well, no. I couldn't because after they asked all these questions about how often I go over to Victoria, if I ever go to the stamp club swaps, and if I could keep an eye out for anything unusual during my trips, by that time I could hardly tell them I'd had the stamps all along. They never asked me if I'd seen them here on the island or I would have told them. Besides, I'm making progress in my crime lab."

"What?!"

"If you'd come over you could see."

"Alyssum, much as I would love to see your . . . your new project, I have to go. Dinner's almost ready."

"Can you come over tomorrow?"

"Maybe. I have to, you know, help around here."

I expect an argument, but instead Alyssum says, "Oh, actually, you can't."

"I can't? Why not?"

"Thursday."

"So?"

"Don't you go to your writing group on Thursdays?"

It's crazy, but a wave of wanting to start bawling again sweeps over me. "Oh . . . yeah."

"Are you okay?"

"I'm fine. I just forgot." Matt has dished out big squares of the lasagna and sliced up the French bread. "I really have to go now."

"Well, call me on Friday, okay? And find out who that woman in black is!"

It's not easy to get Alyssum off the phone once she gets chatting but finally, after I describe what we're having for dinner and insist my meal is getting cold, she hangs up. I'm the last one to sit down at the table. Mom is nowhere to be seen.

Dinner seems to take a thousand years. The scrape and clatter of cutlery against the plates is the only sound except for the loud ticking of the kitchen clock.

All through the meal, noises that should have been background noises get louder and louder until they practically take over.

Writer Girl resists the urge to slap her hands over her ears. She wants to sing out, "I'm not listening—I'm not listening," but her grandmother keeps looking at her so intently, even her silent questions are deafening.

The slosh of juice pouring into my glass is a roaring waterfall, the scritch of Matt's chair on the floor a landslide, and the first spatters of rain outside a tropical monsoon.

Twice Granny looks from me to Dad to the closed door leading to the hallway. Normally, our dinner table is noisy with chatter, Dad's dumb jokes, and Mom telling me and Matt to sit up straight and keep both hands above the table.

"There's enough for Mom." Matt's voice is loud and strained. "Do you think she wants bread, too?"

"Sure," Dad answers. "Put a piece on her plate."

"I'll take it to her," Granny offers. "As a matter of fact, I'll take my dinner along and eat with her. I'm sure she'd like the company."

That's fine by me. I don't want to go anywhere near that dark bedroom. It's creepy how Mom keeps the blinds drawn, how she just lies there without moving, how the plates of food we take her sit untouched on her dresser until someone finally takes them away again.

"Are you ready for tomorrow?" Dad asks me when

Granny leaves the table to take Mom's food to the bedroom. Matt tucks into his meal like there's no tomorrow.

I look at him blankly.

"Your writing group. Don't you have an assignment?"

Everyone, it seems, is on top of my schedule except me.

"I guess. Yes, actually. I haven't finished the new scene . . ." Escape from the table is more and more appealing with each passing minute. Though Dad and Matt are nearly done, I've barely been able to pick at the food on my plate. Writing is a great excuse to get away. I push back my chair, put my plate on the counter and say, "I'd better get going. I have lots to do. . . ."

"You've hardly eaten, Heather."

"I'm fine." Dad doesn't seem convinced. "Really. I'm fine. I'll eat later." He doesn't look like he has the strength to argue.

"Okay. Matt cooked. You do the dishes. Then you can go."

"But—"

"No buts."

I remember the conversation we had earlier about Mia's empty water dish and my help, and let my brilliant arguments about why I shouldn't have to do the dishes die on my lips.

At the sink, with my wrists plunged into the soapy water, I decide to try and think up as many words and phrases as I can relating to the unpleasantness of chores. Real writers take advantage of every moment, every experience, to enrich their work. They use the mundane details of their lives in their writing all the time. It's hard to think of how doing the dishes could ever be interesting enough to include in a story.

People want to read about danger, excitement, and

romance—not soap bubbles and the way our dishwashing brush has a layer of grey scum right at the base of the bristles.

Writer Girl gives the stiff brush a good rinse in very hot water and then plunges her hands into the murky grey swill. Her fingers close around the handle of a carefully honed knife. As she draws it from the bubbly depths of the sink, water trickles from its razor-sharp blade. . . .

In my book, I could have the murder victim get stabbed. I line up several knives, potential murder weapons, on the counter. I pick up a butter knife and push the tip of its blade into my palm. It makes a little round dent but it seems unlikely anyone could do much damage with a weapon like that.

The sharp knife we use for cutting vegetables is another story. The tip is pointy and the blade so sharp that even hefty carrots pose no serious challenge.

I hold the knife lightly in my hand and wonder what it would feel like to push the blade into someone who was still alive. Just the thought of it makes me feel queasy.

Someone would really have to be filled with some horrible kind of hate to actually kill another person. I jab the knife into the air in front of me, imagining how hard I'd actually have to poke at someone to pierce a vital organ. Why on earth does anyone hate the poor farmer in my novel so much they'd stab him with a vegetable knife and stuff his body in a hay manger?

The murderer's motivation has to be pretty realistic, or nobody will believe the story. Do I hate anyone that much? Steffie maybe? I don't like her and I'm mad she made me say mean things to Eric, but I wouldn't ever stab a knife into her. Okay. She didn't force me to behave the way I did, but if she wasn't such a . . .

A more chilling thought presses into my head. What if someone hated *me* so much they would want to kill me? How would I protect myself? I'm not that strong and I don't even have a weapon to use, unless I count the vegetable knife. That's sort of useless since I can hardly stuff that thing in my back pocket and take it to school with me. We don't have security guards here, not like at the big schools in Toronto, but still, I'm sure someone would notice the green handle sticking out of my back pocket and definitely the blood stains if I forgot it was there and sat down too fast. Yuck. Heather, how morbid.

Who would hate me, though? I'm not the sort of person who makes enemies. At least, I never used to be. . . .

Eric's face hovers before me, hurt and humiliated in front of all his friends. Eric, a boy intimately familiar not only with all the many ways a murder could be committed, but also knowledgeable about all the ways criminals can avoid detection.

I toss the sharp knife into the water and watch it disappear beneath the bubbles. Before I can think any more gruesome thoughts, I click on the radio and turn it up loud. Eric is just a boy. A regular kind of boy who writes stories. He's not going to do anything to me. Especially not if I apologize for my stupid remark.

I may not have anything decent written in time for my writing group, but now I have to go to the meeting tomorrow anyway—to protect my health. And, to protect my sanity.

All thoughts of how best to phrase my apology fly from my head when we pull into the parking lot of the Community Centre.

"Got everything?" Dad asks.

I touch my notebook and pen in my bookbag and the plate of cookies in my lap. "I think so."

"I'll be back in two hours. Look out for me, okay?"

The Community Centre is really a big, old wooden house, three stories high with a verandah and surrounded by a huge garden. Out back there's a small adventure playground for the preschool kids and around the other side there's a greenhouse.

The wide stairs leading up to the double-wide front doors are like something from a movie set. In the summer, pots of red, pink, and white geraniums sit on each step. In winter, volunteers move the pots into the big greenhouse.

My hand is on the door handle of the car and I'm ready to get out, when I see her—the woman in the black coat. She's gliding down the stairs, her eyes glittering in the darkness of evening. She turns and hurries around the side of the building, the bottom edge of her coat skimming the gravel of the parking lot.

I let out my breath slowly as she disappears from view.

"Are you going?"

I duck my head down and rummage in my bag, pretending to look for something. The shadows on Dad's face yawn and shift as a set of headlights draws close and then passes by. The other car is a small convertible. It's too dark to see what colour it is, but the elegant shape at the wheel is unmistakable. The Tamolinos woman. The stamp thief.

"There. I found my back-up pen."

"Go on—it's cold out here. I'll see you later."

Chapter Eleven

Collected Quote #19
Fiction is an act of revenge.—John Hawkes

"You're late," Wynd says by way of a welcome when I walk in.

My watch says 7:04. That's hardly enough to worry about but all I say is, "Sorry." Eric is already in his place under the table, Wynd is sprawled on the couch, and Gillian is getting organized in a reclining armchair.

Eric studiously ignores me as I pull a kitchen chair closer to the others. He is telling everyone else about some old woman who fell through a rotten well cover and was trapped on a narrow ledge overnight. Her daughter heard her calling for help the next morning and phoned the Tarragon Island Volunteer Fire Department.

"Imagine if her daughter hadn't come by for a visit," Gillian says. "She might never have been found."

"That's disgusting. Imagine drinking contaminated water!"

"Oh, Wynd—gross."

The room where we meet must once have been a living room—it has high ceilings, huge windows looking out over the garden, and a giant brick fireplace.

"Where's Willow?" Gillian asks, turning away from Wynd who is making gagging motions.

"Babysitting." Eric sounds grumpy, which is not a good thing since his bad mood will only make my job of apologizing more difficult.

Since there's no way I'm going to say anything to Eric in front of the others, I decide to take advantage of our late start and ask about the mysterious woman. I put the plate of cookies on the table and hope my offering will make them feel favourably disposed towards me.

"Ummm . . . does anyone happen to know who that woman was?"

"What woman?" Gillian smoothes her hand over a blank white page in her notebook.

"That tall woman in the black coat who left just before I came in."

"Who's asking?" Eric asks. He manages to make it sound like a supreme challenge, like I've asked something incredibly rude. It occurs to me that however brilliantly I might craft my apology, he might choose not to accept it.

"Was she singing?" Wynd asks with a smirk.

"Shut up," Eric says and shoots an elastic band at her. It wedges in her corkscrew curls and she scowls as she fiddles to free it.

"Singing?"

"Eric's mom is a jazz singer," Gillian says without looking up from the border she's doodling all around the perimeter of her notebook page.

"Eric's mother?"

Eric shoots another elastic, this time at Gillian.

Wynd snorts from the couch. "You can always hear Eric's mom coming a mile away."

I can feel my jaw hanging open. Before it falls right

off, I close my mouth with a soft puff. Eric steadfastly refuses to look at me, which is a good thing, I suppose, or I'd probably get nailed with one of his elastic bands.

"Can't help who we have for mothers, can we?" he says, effectively ending the discussion about his own. "We should get started. Willow said she'd try to get here about eight for the second half. Her parents had to go to a save-the-beaver-colony meeting."

"Is that tonight?" Gillian asks. "I wanted to go to that. Those Wilson brothers don't care about the beavers at all—they just want to divide their property in half and sell. Tough tootsies that the dam is right on the proposed property line."

"Tough tootsies?" Wynd says.

"Can we get started here?" Eric asks.

"I'll go first," Wynd offers. She doesn't wait for agreement. Wynd clears her throat and begins to read from a story she's writing about a plague in which the palms of people's hands and the soles of their feet get painful blisters. That's just the first symptom. Eventually, the victims get lesions all over their bodies and basically burn up with a horrible fever.

Only seven people from this one village survive and they're all weak and fighting over the last of their tinned provisions.

One character in particular, Jeannine, is so realistic I can practically see her.

Jeannine leaned forward, her eyes bugged out with a kind of half-starved madness.

'I should get to keep the tuna. I found the tin.'

Ryan can tell she's getting agitated by the way her chin juts forward with each word she punches towards him.

'You can't just take what you want, Ryan! Not—any—more!'

She jabs her finger in his direction. Her nose reminds him of a sharp chicken beak and he backs off before she can strike at him."

"What's your problem?" Wynd demands, stopping suddenly.

Gillian quivers with giggles on the couch.

"This part isn't funny!"

"Jeannine! I know who that is!"

Eric starts laughing. "You're right!"

Eric emerges from his regular place on the floor to sit beside Wynd on the couch. Reluctantly, she sits up to make room for him. Since Eric is now laughing great, loud, gasping guffaws, Gillian can no longer hold her giggles to a semi-polite twitter. She roars and her pen rolls off her notebook and onto the floor.

"Can—you—believe—it?" Eric stands up and starts stalking around the room like an angry hen. His neck glucks back and forth with each word. With his thumbs in his armpits, he flaps his stubby wings to make a point.

"You've—been—spying—on—me!"

Gillian gets right into the spirit of things and chimes in, "Novelist Wynd Bell imitates island resident in latest book. Victim clucks her displeasure to local lawyer!"

Poor Wynd desperately tries to look fierce, but the corners of her mouth twitch and her shoulders keep giving little telltale jerks.

"Shut up!"

"Brrr—uuck!" Eric clucks and Gillian tips over on her side, clutching her stomach.

I feel like a total foreigner while the three of them cluck and laugh and bug their beady eyes in and out. When their laughter slows a little, I ask, "Who are you talking about?"

Gillian takes pity on me. "You haven't met her yet?"

"Met who?"

"That character, Jeannine, she's just like Marjorie Ellington—the chicken lady."

"Chicken lady? Is she the one who sells eggs on Tiger Lake Road?"

"Eggs? No. Marjorie's a bank teller."

"So why do you call her the chicken lady?"

"When she gets agitated, she acts just like a chicken—just exactly the way Wynd described it. Everybody on Tarragon Island knows about Marjorie Ellington. Oh! Remember when she found out old Benson had been stealing her apples and she nearly pecked him to death at the Saturday market?"

Everybody but me starts laughing hysterically.

"I was there!" Gillian shrieks.

"I heard the paper was going to print a picture of her waving her finger at Benson but she threatened to sue," Eric added.

"Look, I was just doing what we talked about a few weeks ago—you know, observing people closely to get ideas for how they behave, their gestures and stuff."

Eric suddenly looks very serious. "Wynd, for people who live anywhere except Tarragon Island, it's a great description. Fantastic. She really breathes on the page . . . well, clucks on the page." He winks. "Nobody else will know who it is."

Wynd looks a little uneasy. "Maybe I should change it."

"No," Eric says firmly. "It's a great description. Leave it just the way it is."

Wynd's shy smile changes her whole face, softens the hard mask she usually wears and brings a warmth to her eyes that wasn't there before.

"Jeannine snatched the tin of tuna fish back from Ryan's hand. She had spent hours searching through the abandoned school buildings before she'd found anything edible. She'd be damned if she would just hand it over to her arrogant companion."

Willow arrives right near the end of the meeting, just as we're about to start the free-writing exercise. All evening I've been waiting for an opportunity to talk to Eric privately. Since everyone brought work to read, we haven't had a chance for a break.

"Cool hair," Wynd says, referring to a pure white strip of bleached hair that runs like a road divider down the middle of Willow's head.

"You look like a skunk," Gillian giggles from the armchair. She has it fully reclined so she has to lift her head to see over the twin bumps of her red slippers.

"Move over," Willow says to Wynd. Eric plops back down under the table when Willow settles onto the couch. "Do I have time to read?"

Eric checks his watch. "Be quick or we won't have time to free-write."

Still out of breath, Willow pulls her notebook from her black bag and without fuss begins to read.

"Aloysius licked his lips. The girl stood in the shadows of the doorway, her loose sweater drawn tightly around her shoulders. She cast her eyes down to the ground and her pale face was lost to the darkness.

'Will you come with me, Madeline?'

Aloysius smiled with his lips, careful not to reveal his fangs. When the girl looked down like that, her neck stretched pale and lovely before him."

By the time Aloysius moves closer to kiss her and then gulps down half a litre of blood through two

99

neat puncture wounds in Madeline's neck, I am thoroughly freaked out.

Eric wastes no time jumping in with feedback. "I don't know about the line 'he smiled with his lips,'" he says. "Doesn't smiling imply showing your teeth?"

Willow looks a little hurt but makes a note on her page. "What I meant was that he was trying not to show his teeth—you know, so the girl doesn't realize he's a vampire."

"I know what you meant to say, but it didn't seem to come out quite right."

I have to hand it to Eric—he's really good at listening to people read and then figuring out what would make the story better. Except tonight, after my story, he kept his mouth shut and his silence was more irritating than any criticism he might have offered. It would have been better even if he had said something negative about my stabbing scene instead of the way he had responded with a small groan from under the table and nothing further.

I know Eric well enough to know he always has something to say. I wish we could get over our fight because he really is a good writer and even though he sounds like a know-it-all, his feedback is more useful than anyone else's.

All Gillian had to say about my work was "That's pretty good," which was basically a useless comment, even though it made me feel better for just a moment. When I pressed her for an example of what she liked she said, "I love the part about how the knife gets stuck between the slats of the manger. . . . "

Then Wynd said, "Oh, great—another mystery writer," like listening to my story was the biggest waste of time in the whole world.

I don't know why she even comes to the meetings

since half the time it seems like she hates being here.

When Willow is satisfied she's heard enough comments, Eric says, "We don't have a lot of time so let's get started with the free-write. Here's the first word. *Two-faced.*"

He looks up at me for just a second and then we all begin to write.

Two-faced? Who are you calling two-faced? My pen speeds across the page, fuelled by my fury. *Sometimes there are reasons for someone doing a stupid thing. . . .*

I stop scrawling, thinking that since I have to read my work aloud it shouldn't be too personal . . . *the tall girl with the umbrella said with a frown.* The idea, I know, is just to keep on going and so I do. It takes every morsel of self-control I possess to focus on the exercise and incorporate all the dumb words—*geek* from me, *peanut brittle* from Gillian, *headstone* from Willow, and *punk* from Wynd.

When it comes time to share our work with the others, I bristle when I hear what Eric has to offer. I needn't have worried about protecting his feelings— he certainly didn't try too hard to protect mine.

"*The two-faced girl from Ontario sneered at the handsome basketball star. Being with her snobby new friends turned her from being a reasonably nice person to a cow.*"

Wynd sniggers at that part, though I don't think she could know Eric's nasty attack is aimed at me.

Since the next word Eric had to incorporate was *geek*, his story takes a strange turn.

"*Arthur may have been a brilliant team player and as good-looking as they come, and great at chemistry as well, but for some reason certain people at his school thought he was a geek. Geeks aren't nice people. Geeks know how to make poisons in chemistry, the kind of deadly toxin that could be dusted over a batch of peanut brittle. The victim could eat six chunks of toxic-coated peanut brittle without ever getting suspicious. Arthur didn't have a lot of unsuspecting enemies, or any other kind of enemies, because he knew how to take care of people who bothered him.*

For as long as Arthur had people to annoy him, the headstone-maker in town was happy because business was very, very good. Punk or geek, it didn't matter—Arthur was a happy man when his last enemy was eliminated."

When he folds his paper over at the end of his reading I can hardly stay still in my seat. Eric is clearly a nasty, scum-filled, rotten, putrid nitwit and I can't believe I ever felt sorry for being mean to him. I fume silently through the rest of the meeting, hardly hearing what the others read, and stumble through my own free-write story like I have marbles in my mouth.

Any idea I ever had of apologizing is completely gone when, a little later, we stand on the front steps waiting for our parents to come and get us.

"I had no idea you were brilliant at chemistry," I say coldly.

"I'm not," he answers. "I just like making up stories."

He leaps off the steps when his ride arrives, leaving me sputtering with irritation on the Community Centre porch. Sure enough, it is the mysterious woman with the long coat who is behind the wheel. When Eric opens the passenger door, a whoosh of music spills out into the dark parking lot, a song I don't recognize, something sad with a wailing saxophone and loud drums.

Writer Girl stands motionless in the pool of light cast by the porch light. Her right hand lifts slightly, as if she wants to wave, to call back the tall woman and her angular son. She drinks in the sounds of the night, the thwunk of the car door closing, the muffled music, the popping crinkle of car tires across the gravel, the wind scraping through the vine growing up the side of the porch.

Her intense dislike for the boy prevents her from moving. She balls her right hand into a tight fist and shoves it deep into her sweatshirt pocket.

My curiosity about Eric's mother and why she would steal stamps battles with my growing impatience with Skateboard Boy. Not only does he think he knows more about writing than anyone, he's quite willing to use his pen to publicly humiliate me when our arguments should be kept private. As Granny says, it's not good form to hang out your dirty laundry in public.

It figures, really. I mean if his mother is a thief, it makes sense he wouldn't think like kids from decent families.

Chapter Twelve

Collected Quote #78
The cruelest lies are often told in silence.
—Robert Louis Stevenson

I'm still seething while I stand outside on the porch of the Community Centre waiting for Dad to arrive. I'm just about ready to turn and go back inside to phone home when a pea green VW van pulls into the parking lot. I recognize it as the Cranwells'. Mrs. Cranwell leans over and opens the passenger door for me. "Hi, Heather."

An ice-cold dread spills through my veins. I can't even form words around the questions whirling through the fog in my head. The door clicks shut but Mrs. Cranwell doesn't drive off right away.

"Heather, it's your grandmother."

Before she has a chance to finish, my throat closes up, muffling a choking sound.

"What happened?"

I press my hands together and wedge them between my knees to stop them from shaking.

"Heather—I'm so sorry. She collapsed."

Collapsed. The word sounds like it's folding in on itself. *She collapsed. She collapsed.* The phrase repeats itself over and over in my head until the words don't sound real at all.

"Where is she?" I manage to ask.

"At the hospital. Your father is with her."

"But what happened?"

"She just collapsed."

We're going in circles.

"We don't know why. Apparently she said her heart . . ."

"Her heart?" There was nothing wrong with Granny's heart. There couldn't be.

"Can I see her?"

I don't want Granny to die before I get to say goodbye. I don't want it to be like Grandpa. "Why?" I ask, and then my cheeks are wet with tears and Mrs. Cranwell has slipped the van into gear and we're driving through the darkness towards home.

"Where's Mom?" I ask as we pull up in front of the house. I wipe my dribbling nose on the back of my hand.

"She's waiting with Matt. I'm going to take her to the hospital after I drop you off."

"We have to stay here alone?"

"Alyssum's here. I'll be back soon."

"Why can't we come, too?"

"I'm sorry, Heather—until they know how ill your Granny is . . . come on, your mom is waiting."

I swing my legs from the van and plod up the steps. I can hardly move and the back door seems six times heavier than normal.

"Mom?" It's all I can manage to say before I start crying again. Mom is halfway into her jacket and awkwardly reaches out to touch my hair. Her face is a horrible shade of grey and her eyes are red.

"Dad just called. They're doing tests. Granny's okay. She's resting. I'll phone as soon as I know anything."

Her sentences are slow and deliberate but her gaze

flicks from Matt and Alyssum at the table to me to Mrs. Cranwell standing near the door. She shrugs the rest of the way into her coat and moves towards the door.

"Mrs. Cranwell will be back soon. Everything will be okay." Her voice quivers and she turns quickly into the darkness outside. Mrs. Cranwell gives us a little wave and follows her.

Collapse. Writer Girl stands in the middle of a grand marble hallway. She watches as first an old man and then an old woman, and finally her own mother, slowly buckle at the knees and sink to the cool, white floor.

"Heather?"

Alyssum sounds unsure of herself. I turn and for the first time take in the table properly. There's a big plate of cookies in the middle as well as a stack of playing cards. Three hands of cards lie fanned on the table, one each in front of Matt and Alyssum, and one in front of Mom's now empty chair.

"What happened?" I ask Matt.

When he answers his voice is flat, unhappy.

"We were making cookies. . . ."

"You and Granny?"

"Mm. And then she started breathing funny and she put her hands like this. . . ." He puts his hands over his chest. "She got all pale and I yelled and Mom came out of the bedroom and told me to get Dad so I ran to the studio and when we got back Mom had called 911 and Granny was lying on the floor."

The cold feeling of horror is back and I sit at Mom's place and fold her cards. "Were her eyes open?" Alyssum looks at me like I'm crazy. "I mean, did she pass out or faint or something?"

Matt shakes his head. "I don't think so. Granny kept saying not to fuss, that she was fine, something about having one of her spells."

"What kind of spells?" I hadn't seen any sign of spells, whatever that was supposed to mean. Granny had been a whirl of activity ever since her arrival. Her latest project had been to paint the shelves in the linen closet. For two days the hallway had been filled with piles of towels and tablecloths.

Matt shrugs. "I dunno. The ambulance people put a plastic mask on her face and made her lie on a stretcher."

"We should do something, I guess." Since I'm the oldest and in charge, at least until Mrs. Cranwell gets back, I feel obliged to keep the younger kids occupied.

"More cards?" Alyssum suggests.

"Sure." I'm not much of a card player but doing something, anything, is better than sitting around speculating about what happened to Granny.

"We can play Fish," Matt says, flipping the cards into messy piles in front of each of us.

"Hey!" I pull my feet back and peer under the table. Mia and Sandy, are locked in mortal combat. Sandy is about ten times the size of Mia, but that doesn't stop the fierce little terrier from snarling viciously at the bigger dog. She nips at one of Sandy's ears and Sandy plops her paw right over Mia's head to pin her to the ground.

I smile—I can't help myself. What a pair of goofs.

"Ready?" Matt asks.

I pick up my cards and sort them quickly.

"Have you got an eight?" Matt asks.

Alyssum groans and slides a card across the table to my brother. Our game continues, interrupted occasionally by muffled woofs from under the table until Matt slaps a pair of kings on the table and says, "Hah!" He's never been a gracious winner.

I play on with a concentrated intensity that has

107

more to do with blocking out intruding hospital thoughts than it does with trying to win at cards. We talk very little, as if conversation about Granny would be too dangerous and small talk would be disrespectful.

Alyssum has just dealt the third or fourth hand when Mrs. Cranwell pushes in through the kitchen door. We all look at her, the game instantly forgotten.

"She'll be fine," Mrs. Cranwell says before we can ask. "It wasn't a heart attack."

"How long . . ." The phone cuts off Matt's question. We all look at each other dumbly as the phone rings a second time. *Get up and answer the phone.* The words seem so loud it's like I've spoken them aloud.

"Hello?"

"Hi, Heather."

"Dad—how is she?"

"She'll be okay. The doctor wants to keep her in overnight and run a few more tests tomorrow. Granny should be home by the time you get home from school."

"School?" The stove clock says it's nearly one in the morning.

"You can sleep in a little in the morning. We'll drive you when we come back to the hospital. You and Matt should go to bed. Mom and I will be home soon."

After he hangs up I turn back to the expectant faces around the table. "I don't know," I say. "It wasn't a heart attack. She'll be home tomorrow."

As I get ready for bed there is one disturbing question that rattles persistently around and around in my head. If Granny hadn't had a heart attack, then what was wrong with her? People don't just collapse for no reason. *Collapse.* That word again.

108

Writer Girl collapses into bed. Though the hour is late, her eyes remain open. She stares at the dim outline of her window so long it begins to shimmer until it eventually disintegrates and disappears.

"Heather?"

"Already?" I stuff my head under the pillow and try to find my way back into sleep.

"Come on—your alarm didn't go off."

I must have forgotten to turn it on.

"You don't want to be late for school."

Actually, I wouldn't mind being late for school. I wouldn't mind never going back to school. The weight of everything I have to do today makes my head pound.

"Come on, Heather—make a noise."

I make a noise like a dying elephant.

"That's better."

It's not until I hear the door close and Dad's footsteps retreating that I realize I didn't tell Alyssum about my discovery about Eric's mother. No matter what happens, I promise myself that later today I will go to her house to fill her in.

In the car, I gnaw on a bagel. We really did sleep late and there's no time for a proper breakfast at home. Mom couldn't wait—she staggered out to the old farm truck and drove to the hospital without us. The thought of the dark bags under her eyes and coffee mug in her hand sends a shudder through me. She looked awful as she drove off. I wonder if she even remembered to brush her hair.

Alyssum's mom arrived at the house just as we were

leaving. She'll be there when Matt gets up and together they'll feed and water the animals. Milly and Dr. deBoer will be at the clinic by nine. Mom's part-time partner seems to be getting used to handling most of Mom's appointments as well as his own.

"Mom's going to go out of business."

Dad snaps off the radio. "Not likely. People do get sick, you know. Even vets. Brian can handle things for the next couple of weeks until your mother and your grandmother are back on their feet."

"A couple of weeks? Is Granny that sick? Is Mom?"

Dad shakes his head. "Your mother is really struggling to hold everything together. Granny was . . . well, what happened to her was a real shock to your mom."

Dad sighs and stares intently into the rain. He adjusts the speed of the wiper and turns up the fan so the window defogs faster. "She was very depressed even before this happened."

I think of how Mom hasn't been eating, how she's barely spoken to us, how she keeps trying to go to work but winds up drifting into bed.

"If your mother doesn't take some time off and look after herself . . . well, she'll be no use to anyone."

It's hard to believe we are talking about my mother, the successful vet, the woman everyone calls when their cats are sick or when they need somewhere to leave their python when they go on vacation—my mother who loves to eat Matt's chocolate cake. She is just not the sort of person who gets so overwhelmed with life that she can't get up in the morning. She loves her work. It doesn't make any sense.

"So what happened to Granny?" Dad looks distinctly uncomfortable. He shifts in his seat and tugs on his ear.

"It seems she had palpitations."

"Palpa what?"

"Palpitations. That's when your heart starts pounding like crazy."

"So it was her heart?"

"No, though Granny said it felt like her heart was going to explode. She got so scared she hyperventilated."

"Breathed too fast?"

Dad nods. "Then she felt faint and that made her even more scared and that made her heart pound harder. She thought she was having a heart attack and she got even more terrified. She panicked. Your mom panicked."

"But why did she have those palpitations in the first place?"

"The doctor said it's not unusual for someone who is under a lot of stress to have something called a panic attack."

"Panic attack?"

"Granny said she's had several since Grandpa died but none were as bad as yesterday."

"So it was all in her head?"

Dad doesn't answer right away. Like my hand has a mind of its own, it floats forward and turns the radio back on. The news blares at us and my fingers go numb.

"Well, the doctor explained it by saying how our bodies and minds are not as separate as we like to think. When we're really worried or upset often our bodies react, too."

I burst into tears. Is everybody in my family going crazy? Who's going to be next, I wonder? I thump the inside of the car door with my fist, over and over again.

We pull into the three-car parking lot behind Andrea's House of Heavenly Bagels and Dad waits patiently while I blow my nose and get my shaking shoulders under control.

"We'll have a coffee and then I'll take you to school, okay?"

"No! I don't want to go to school! Can't I see Granny? I want to see for myself that she's okay."

He looks confused. "I just don't know, Heather."

I feel like hitting him. He's supposed to know what to do. I clench my fists inside the pockets of my fleece jacket.

"Why shouldn't I see her?"

"I don't want to upset her."

"Why would it upset her to see me?" Dad has no answer to that.

The minute we get inside Andrea's bagel place and sit down, I realize it was a big mistake to come in. This isn't like a good old Toronto coffee shop visit. Dad keeps looking at the bagel-shaped clock behind the register and I hardly even taste my steamed milk. We don't talk at all and the silence is really awful.

"Please let me see Granny. If I can see her then I'll go to school," I say, though I don't feel like I have much influence on what's going to happen.

Dad sighs and swirls the dregs of his coffee around and around in his cup. "Okay. Let's go."

Chapter Thirteen

Granny's hospital room has two beds in it, though
the second one is empty. When we walk in Granny
turns her head towards us and smiles sheepishly. She
pats a spot beside her on the bed and I sit down.

"Oh dear, what a muddle," she says. "How silly to
get everyone so worked up over nothing."

I don't think it's nothing when you think your
heart is going to explode.

"Are you coming home today?"

"I certainly hope so. The food here is dreadful. How
anyone can make such a mess of scrambled eggs, I'll
never know." We smile and that's when I notice Mom
sitting in an armchair in front of the big window on
the other side of the room. She's watching something
outside.

A grey squirrel flits from branch to branch of a
cedar tree, its twitching tail held like a furry umbrella
over its head each time it stops to nibble at
something small and brown it holds between its front
paws.

It seems ludicrous that under the circumstances we
are all watching the wildlife. I want to be mad at

Mom, but seeing her dark hair falling messily over her creamy-coloured sweater scares me. She looks pale and weak, a lot sicker than Granny. I wish I knew some sort of magic to make her turn and smile at me.

"I'm on my way to school," I say to fill the silence.

It seems like a big effort for Mom to turn from the window and when she does I can see just how exhausted she looks.

"That's good, Heather. We have to keep on keeping on."

It's eerie to hear one of Grandpa's sayings coming out of Mom's mouth.

She tries to smile but it's a feeble effort. Her voice is soft and raspy, like she's coming down with a cold. All I can think of is getting out of the hospital room as fast as possible before I start bawling again. Granny takes my hand and gives it a squeeze. "The doctor says I should start meditating!" she says. Despite myself I giggle. I can't imagine Granny sitting still long enough to do any deep breathing. I wonder whether that would be enough to stop her panic attacks.

I stand up to go and Mom says, "We'll see you later, Heather."

Dad raises his eyebrows at me and I give him a quick nod. Now that I'm here, I feel pretty desperate to leave again. This is not a happy room.

"I'll be back soon, you two," Dad says, and he gestures to me to leave. "I'll just drive Heather to school."

"Hurry back before they try to feed me again!" Granny quips with a groan and a chuckle.

There's no response from Mom. She's staring out the window again, even though the squirrel seems to have disappeared.

Out in the parking lot the rain has started again in earnest and we hurry to the car.

"Are you sure you are up to going to school?" Dad asks.

I shrug. "Better than sitting around at home."

He fires up the engine and cranks up the heat.

"When will Mom feel better? Why aren't the pills working? Is she still taking those antidepressants? Why does she still look so sad?"

"Heather, slow down! She is taking the pills but they take a while to kick in. Sometimes it can be several weeks before you notice a difference. Sometimes they have to try a couple of different kinds of medication before they find the one that will help."

This doesn't sound very promising. What if there isn't a kind of pill to help Mom? What then? Surely people don't just go to bed and stay there forever?

"What about Granny? Will she keep panicking?"

"The psychiatrist is coming to see her later today. He's going to talk to her and assess how she's doing. There are various techniques she can try. But if the panic attacks keep happening . . ." He pauses like he doesn't want to go on but I guess what he was about to say.

"There are probably pills she can take, right?" I can't believe my whole family is turning into a pack of drug addicts.

"Yes, as a matter of fact, there is medication she can take. The doctor thinks that might not be necessary."

"What if Mom doesn't get un-depressed?" I don't like the way Dad grips the steering wheel like he's trying to squeeze the life out of it.

"Well, the worst-case scenario would be that she would have to go to a special hospital over on

Vancouver Island. Just for a while."

"You mean a mental hospital? A place for psychos?"

"Don't talk like that. Your mother is not psycho. A psychiatric hospital is not a bad place for a person to be. It's a last resort, though. Most likely she'll be on the mend before we know it. We just have to be patient."

Since Dad sounds pretty vague, like he's not exactly sure of what's going on himself, there's no point in pushing for more details. I make a mental note to have a look at the library book he talked about as soon as possible.

"Are you sure you're okay?" he asks as we pull up in front of the school. "Because we haven't really had time to . . . you know . . . to talk. It's been hard—for all of us. I remember how difficult it was for me when my brother had the accident. . . ."

"I'm fine." My voice comes out sounding positively fierce, though inside, I'm glad he asked. I don't want to hear about my uncle's sailing accident, though. There's enough misery to think about without dredging up the worst moment in my dad's child-hood, too. I take a deep breath to try to quell the wobbliness I feel and say, "What do I write in the late book?"

"Say you slept in—that's the truth. You don't need to say why if you don't want to."

Right—like I would want to walk into the office and say, "Guess what? My grandmother thinks her heart is exploding and my mom is so depressed she might be crazy enough to lock away—please excuse me for being a little late."

Mr. Bell is busy sorting lunch orders in the office when I walk in to sign the book. I take my father's advice and write, "Slept in." Mr. Bell doesn't interro-

116

gate me or anything. He doesn't even look mildly suspicious. He just nods and says, "You'd better hurry up—you can still catch the second half of your class."

School drags. All day long every minute seems to take an hour. I am torn in half. Part of me wants to go to the office and phone home to get someone to pick me up. The other half of me doesn't want to be near my house or my family and dreads the end of the day when I'll have to face them. The clocks in every class-room pause between seconds, their hands stuck, reluctant to move on.

"Hey, space cadet," Steffie says when the lunch bell goes. "You coming?"

I shake my head. The last thing I want to do is hang out with Steffie and Co. "I have to go see Ms. Thompsen about the English class I missed this morning."

"Sleep in?"

"Hung over." I have no idea why I say that except maybe it will get Steffie off my case and explain why I look so awful.

"Cool," Steffie says approvingly. "There's a party at my place this weekend—my parents are going to Vancouver. Do you want to come?"

"Maybe. I'm kind of grounded at the moment."

"Come on, Steff!" Alicia yells from the other end of the hallway.

Steffie gives me a last, questioning look and then turns and stalks off to join her friends.

The meeting with Ms. Thompsen takes all of five minutes. It turns out I didn't miss too much—an in-class essay I can do over the weekend. "Would it be okay to stay in here and eat?"

The teacher takes a long look at me and asks, "Is everything okay?"

My bottom lip quivers. "Not exactly. I just don't feel like . . . I just don't want to socialize." I wonder if she's going to press me for a reason and I wish I hadn't asked to stay inside.

Writer Girl watches the tall, slightly awkward teacher absent-mindedly nudging a row of paper clips into perfect alignment with the tip of a Mickey Mouse pencil. The teacher's short, black hair is speckled through with flecks of grey. Salt and pepper hair.

"Sure. I'll close the door after I leave. Nobody will bother you."

"Thanks." I breathe a huge sigh of relief when the classroom door closes after her. So far, Ms. Thompsen is my favourite teacher here.

So that's how I spend my lunch hour—sitting in Ms. Thompsen's deserted classroom on the second floor, staring out the window at the red-gold branches of a giant arbutus tree arching up into the rain.

Chapter Fourteen

Collected Quote #9
In the deepest heart of all of us there is a corner in which
the ultimate mystery of things works sadly.—William James

"We're going over to Alyssum's," Matt says when I
walk in the door after school.

"Right now?"

He nods and grins. "Lasagna. Vegetarian lasagna. I
helped Alyssum's mom grate the cheese this afternoon."

"Where is everyone?"

He knows who I mean. "At the hospital. Granny's
been having heart tests and stuff all day. It took
longer than they thought. Dad was here for a while to
do the chores and then he went back to the hospital.
All we have to do is make sure the chickens are in and
feed the girls."

The "girls" are Matt's two cows—Jinnie and Chelsea.

"Granny should be home early this evening."

I think of her propped up in the hospital bed,
trying to make jokes. I guess she'll be mad that she
had to eat two more meals' worth of hospital food.
"Have you seen Mom?"

"Nope. She stayed at the hospital all day."

"Can we do the girls now? Then we can go."

Matt nods. "You can see the costumes. Alyssum
and I worked on them some more today."

119

"Okay." I smile at Matt and nod even though I couldn't care less about his dumb costume. It is a good thing we're going over to Alyssum's, though—I can finally talk to her about Eric's mother.

"Who's going to wash?" Alyssum's mother asks.

"I will," I volunteer. I like washing the dishes better than drying because then I'm done first.

"Thanks, Heather. Matt and Alyssum, you can both help dry. I'm going to give the boys a bath."

Mrs. Cranwell takes each of the twins, Robert and Eric, by the hand and they all toddle off to the bathroom.

The minute her mother leaves the room, Alyssum turns to me. "Guess what?" she says.

"What?"

"I found out something about the boxes!"

"The Tamolinos boxes?"

She nods furiously. "The fingerprints don't match!"

"Fingerprints?"

"Wash faster! I'll show you."

I've never scrubbed lasagna dishes quicker. In fifteen minutes all the dishes are washed, dried, and neatly stacked in the cupboards and Alyssum, Matt, and I are in Alyssum's bedroom, staring at a most amazing display.

"How did you do this?"

Lined up on her large worktable are six pieces of white card and on each of the cards are several black fingerprints. Under each fingerprint Alyssum has neatly stuck a sticky note labelled with the letter *A*, *B*, or *C*. She picks up a file folder from beside the cards and takes out a sheet of paper filled with notes.

"The Internet is so great," Alyssum says. "Did you know you can order a full fingerprint lifting kit for just $25.95 US?"

I lean over to get a closer look at the row of finger-prints.

"You ordered a fingerprint kit from your computer?"

"Sure. I told Mom I really, really wanted to start a unit on crime science and after that, it was easy. I ordered two books and this fingerprinting kit. The books arrived yesterday and the kit today. I've been busy."

"So, what do the letters mean?"

Alyssum is happy to explain. "Each letter stands for a suspect."

"Suspect?"

"Anyone who touched the boxes."

"That must have been a lot of people—the clerk in the lingerie shop, the person who bought the box, who may or may not have been the same person with the stamp collection, the thief . . ."

My head spins with the possibilities.

"I was looking for matches between both boxes."

The two Tamolinos boxes are on the table, their glossy surfaces now dirty with some kind of powder. One of them has a big letter *S* beside it.

"What does the *S* mean," Matt asks.

"Stolen. That's the one with the Russian stamps in it."

"So *NS* means 'not stolen'?"

"Right." Alyssum nods officiously at Matt. "So anyway, Suspect A has fingerprints all over the Not Stolen box and the Stolen Box."

"So that's who did it?"

"Shhh. Suspect B also has prints all over the Stolen Box. The clearest prints in both cases are two thumbprints I found on the lids. See Exhibit A." Alyssum points to the first card.

The black prints are clear as anything on the white card. This makes sense since most people would pick up the flattish boxes with their thumbs on top. It's easy to see the two sets of thumbprints belong to two different people. One set has swirly spirals and the other looks like a series of arches, one nested inside the other.

"There are a couple of other people's prints on one box or the other but not both. I figure those are probably from two different sales clerks and maybe from you, too."

It's a little shocking to know my fingerprints are on the evidence. Alyssum doesn't seem too worried, though, as she busily ploughs on with the report of her investigation.

"Suspect C also has prints all over both boxes."

"This is hopeless!" I say. "How are you possibly going to sort this out if everyone has touched the Stolen Box?"

Alyssum smirks. "Suspect C is easily eliminated since Suspect C is me. This is where it gets interesting. . . ."

"See the inside of the Stolen Box?" She puts on a pair of light cotton gloves and lifts the lid of the box. Inside is the folder with the clear plastic cover, the folder containing the pages with the Russian stamps.

"The plastic cover of the folder was great for picking up prints. Only two of the suspects had their prints both on the inside and on the outside of the box."

"Who?"

"Suspect B and Suspect C."

"You and . . . one of the people who touched both Tamolinos boxes."

"Right. There's also another print that's on the cover of the folder but not on the outside of the box. That belongs to Suspect D."

"Who would that be?"

"I wasn't sure, so then I decided to have a look at the stamps in the Not Stolen box because I had an idea that the collector of all these stamps must have handled things somewhere along the way."

This was all getting very complicated.

"Why didn't you check the Russian stamps for fingerprints?"

Alyssum gives me one of her "I can't believe you are really this dumb" looks and continues. "Stamp collectors don't touch their stamps. They use tongs."

"So what good would it do to check the stamps in the Not Stolen box?"

"Because those stamps are still stuck to the corners of envelopes. Collectors can touch the envelopes, just not the stamps."

She looks unbelievably pleased with herself. I can just see how the next step is going to be Alyssum setting up the Cranwell Detective Agency.

"So?"

"So, I dusted several of the envelopes and found two clear samples that exactly match the prints on the cover of the Russian collection. My guess is those prints belong to the stamp collector."

"So why aren't they on the outside of the boxes?"

"Maybe the stamp collector isn't the one to put the stamps in the Tamolinos boxes."

The three of us stare at the evidence in front of us, trying to piece together what it all means.

"So," Matt says slowly, "the most likely thief is Suspect B?"

Alyssum nods.

"Why?" I ask. Somehow my mind can't seem to work this logically. I'm still getting over the fact Alyssum had the nerve to order fingerprint dusting stuff off the Internet. Matt doesn't seem to have any trouble keeping it all straight in his head.

"Well, Suspect A didn't touch the Russian folder. Suspect D seems to have handled all the stamps but not the boxes. That's probably the owner of the collection. The thief must have handled at least the stolen box since it was carried to the school and it makes sense the thief would also have touched the Russian folder since that was the valuable one and they'd want to examine their haul. We can eliminate Suspect C since that's Alyssum."

"This is all very interesting," I say. "But what if I tell you that I know at least one of the people who touched the Not Stolen box."

Now I have the full attention of both Alyssum and Matt.

"Who?"

"Eric's mother! I found out who she is last night at my writer's group."

"Why on earth would Eric's mother want to steal stamps?" Alyssum's eyebrows push together. "Angelica Maloney is a jazz singer. I remember when she and Eric moved here from New York City. I think she's pretty successful—I mean, she has CDs around and stuff. Mom and Dad bought a couple when she moved here. Why would she steal stamps?"

I shrug. "Just because someone's a singer doesn't mean she couldn't be a criminal, too."

"There's more," Alyssum says.

"More prints?"

"No. I called the stamp shop in Victoria, the one where I always take the stamps to sell."

"And?"

"We were talking about rare stamps and collectors here on the island and he asked if I knew anything about the theft of the rare stamps."

"What did you tell him?"

"I said I had heard about the robbery and that I would have loved to have seen those Russian stamps because they must have been interesting."

"What did he say?"

"It was really strange. He said that it wasn't often you talk about Russian stamps twice in one week. Apparently, last week a man called to ask Bill if he knew how much a set of Russian revolutionary stamps would be worth."

"People probably call all the time to ask about stuff like that. . . ."

"They do. But it was still a funny coincidence. Bill thought so, too. All the big stamp dealers had been contacted by the police in case someone tried to sell the missing stamps."

"Didn't he ask who was calling?" Matt asks.

"Of course. The minute he did, the guy on the phone got all nervous and hung up."

"That must have been the thief!" Matt says.

"Maybe. Since the person who called was a man . . . and if that person has anything to do with the stolen stamps . . . well, all we know for sure is that person can't be Eric's mother."

"What about his father?"

"He doesn't have one."

"Everyone has a father," Matt says knowingly. "They are biological necessities."

Alyssum rolls her eyes. "Duh. I guess he has one somewhere. When they moved here, it was just Eric, his mother, and I think maybe his grandfather. I remember Eric sat beside an old man at a concert his mother gave right around the time they moved here. That was about two years ago, I think. I've seen the old man with them since then—at the Saturday market."

I shake my head. "Fine, but how on earth is this going to help us figure out who stole the stamps? And we really have no idea why a thief would want to put the stamps in a donation box instead of trying to sell them. We don't even know who they belonged to in the first place. We don't know much, in fact."

"Crime investigations take time," Alyssum says. "Just write down everything you learn—every little detail helps."

It seems to me we've hit a dead end since we hardly have access to RCMP fingerprint files so we have no idea who Suspects A, B, or D might be.

"Well, Sherlock? What do we do next?" I raise an eyebrow in what I hope is a look that clearly tells Alyssum that the logical thing to do here is turn the evidence over to the police now and forget about being detectives. None of us is any good at it.

Alyssum fixes me with a no-nonsense stare.

"WE wait to hear what YOU find out from Eric."

"What?!"

Alyssum looks quite disappointed with me. "Obviously he's going to know something, like why his mother has her prints all over the Tamolinos boxes."

"She's a singer. Singers always wear fancy underpants."

Matt snorts.

"Shut up."

"Shut up yourself."

For the moment, anyway, there doesn't seem to be

any more to do to solve the great stamp theft mystery. Never at a loss for something to do, Alyssum throws open her closet door and hauls out two huge, floppy structures bigger than she is.

"What the. . . ?"

"Salt . . . and . . . pepper."

"Oh boy . . . those are pathetic!"

The Halloween costumes look nothing like salt and pepper shakers. The chicken wire frames are floppy and sort of caving in where Alyssum and Matt have started to add papier mâché. The surface area still left to cover is huge. I doubt there's any way they're going to be able to finish in time for trick-or-treating.

"Maybe you should think of different costumes."

"They'll be fine," Matt says grimly. "We just have to finish covering the frames. . . ."

"The frames are falling over!"

"She's right," Alyssum concedes. "We're going to find some way to make them stiffer. Right, Matt?"

"Right."

With the two of them standing there side by side with their floppy over-sized hose nozzles I don't have the heart to tell them there's no way their project is going to work. Who am I to say? I'm not even bothering to put on a funny hat.

"When will you see Eric again?"

"Monday. And then only if we happen to trip over each other at school—which is not likely. So, Thursday night at the writing group, I guess."

"That's not soon enough," Alyssum says. "You're right—we can't hold on to these stamps for much longer. I know I'm going to have to turn them over, but it seems like we've just about solved the crime—don't you think?"

"I don't know about that. A close-to-being-solved

127

crime is still an unsolved crime."

Alyssum points her finger at me and fires a pretend gun. I'm not intimidated by her tough display—she's taking the whole detective thing too far.

"I'm not going to phone Eric and ask him over. There's no reason in the world to do that."

Alyssum doesn't seem to have a ready argument so instead she changes the subject. "We have time to add more papier mâché to these. Do you want to help us?"

"Fine."

So that's what we do for the rest of the evening. We mix endless bowls of flour and water sludge, tear up newspapers, and layer soppy strips onto the chicken wire frames. It's not exactly my idea of a thrilling evening, but the steady work and Matt and Alyssum's chatter help keep me from thinking about Mom and Granny.

Chapter Fifteen

Collected Quote #45
Footfalls echo in the memory
Down the passage which we did not take
Towards the door we never opened
Into the rose garden.—T.S. Eliot

Dove Cottage
It's cold out here at night but I like coming to Dove Cottage because it's like a whole other world out here. There's no noise, for one thing. Well, not like TV noise— just the wind and sometimes I can hear the animals moving around in the barn or mooing or clucking.

I push aside my journal. I'm just procrastinating by writing in it. I should really be answering Maggie's letter. I've read it three times already but I don't think I can answer it properly until I've read it a few more times.

The candle flames flicker and I shudder. Dove Cottage looks cozy, but it's pretty leaky—not the roof, it's dry inside, but the wind sneaks in through the cracks in the walls and around the window. When a particularly big gust whooshes past, the curtains move in and out. I found an old pair of green wool gloves and cut the ends out of the fingers so I can still hold my pen. I look like an orphan from a hundred years ago.

I tug the letter from inside my jacket pocket and smooth it out on the desk.

Dear Heather,

Thank you for your letter. It was great to hear from you. I'm sorry to hear about your grandfather. I remember when we went to the farm and you fell in the duck pond and your grandfather told you to hose yourself off and instead you jumped in the cows' water trough and then he got all mad because of all the mud and weeds and stuff that got in the drinking water. Remember?

Of course I remember that trip. It was the last time Maggie and I had been to the farm together. Grandpa had been so mad. He said the milk would go sour if the cows drank dirty water. I don't know if that was actually true or not, but he made me drain out all the water from the trough, scrub it out, and then stand there while I filled the whole thing up again with the hose.

Maggie thought the whole thing was hilarious. I didn't. I was too wet and cold and embarrassed to find anything funny about it at all.

Thinking about it now, what I mostly wish is that I'd never gone near the pond in the first place. It was one of three places we weren't supposed to go on the farm—the other two were near the big pieces of equipment and in the bull's field. Funny, I was never tempted to visit old Boris.

The next part of Maggie's letter is a little strange. She started to write one thing and then scratched it out very thoroughly so there was no way to read through the scribbles. Then she tried again and wrote,

It's hard to tell from your letter whether you like this Eric boy or not. You say he's a good writer and is the only nice

person at school (or, at least that he talked to you when other people didn't). So, I don't really understand why you were so mean to him since it sounds like Steffie and her friends are kind of a bunch of losers.

The next part of the letter makes me want to scream with embarrassment.

I wasn't sure what to think about everything so I told my mom what you wrote. She just asked me if I knew of a single person (including me) who had never ever said or done something mean to somebody else. I thought about that and I guess I can't think of anybody who is perfect and I already know for sure you aren't perfect, so I don't know why I feel like I'm mad at you. I don't even know why I should feel mad because I don't even know Eric.

I'm waiting for your next letter because I think probably you will tell me that you apologized or made it up to him somehow and that's about the best thing you could do at this point. Then again, maybe if he won't talk to you or something you won't be able to apologize and I am not sure if I'll stay mad at you forever or not. I don't think so because I've been mad at you before (remember when we were little and you cut all the hair off my favourite stuffed orangutan?) and I got over it.

So, for now, I guess we are still best friends, unless you don't want to be any more. Either way, I can say anything to you if I'm being honest and that's why I'm going to say that I think the dumbest thing you've done is to start smoking. All the other stuff I kind of understand how it happened, but why would you ever start that disgusting habit? You know how I feel about smokers.

It's true. I know exactly how she thinks about smokers. She hates cigarette smoke and she doesn't care who knows about it, either. I put my head down

131

on my desk. I know that no matter what anyone had said, or how they had teased her or made her feel stupid, Mags would never have smoked. I remind myself that I didn't actually take a puff of a cigarette either, but since Maggie thinks I did, it doesn't make any difference.

Her letter is so confusing. I know she's trying to understand why I said mean things and why I'm supposedly smoking and all of that and she's still trying to be my friend. But I know from the way she wrote that she really doesn't like the things I'm doing. I don't blame her. I don't like the things I'm doing either.

I want to write to her about Mom and how she's so depressed and how I'm really mad at her for being selfish. I want to let her know how scared I am that Granny's heart might actually explode and how I don't think I can deal with one more thing going wrong. I want to write about how the library book on depression says some people get so sad they don't think they can go on living so they kill themselves and how if Mom ever tried that I would be so mad I'd want to kill her myself.

But I know if I write about all that stuff it will sound like I'm making excuses for behaving like an idiot. Besides, how on earth can I even think about writing those things down? I don't want anybody to know about my crazy thoughts or my psycho mother or even Granny who worries so much inside it makes her feel like her heart is blowing up. Not even my best friend needs to know any of that.

I read the letter again. It's like pinching myself really hard, or pulling out hairs one at a time from my head to see if I can make myself cry. I know that what Maggie says about confronting Eric is right. No matter how much I don't like his arrogant ways or how he was mean by writing things about me and then reading them to the group, it doesn't matter. I hurt his feelings and I probably would have done the same thing if the shoe had been on the other foot and he had picked on me first.

I wrap my arms around myself and rub my hands quickly up and down. I'm so cold I can hardly think. There's no point in answering Maggie's letter yet. She's expecting to hear how I've made things better.

Writer Girl wants to kick herself for being so immature. It should be easy to do the right thing, even if that seems highly unpleasant. So why, Writer Girl wonders, does even the thought of taking action seem as appealing as . . . as swallowing live tadpoles?

Chapter Sixteen

Collected Quote #24
Writers seldom choose as friends those self-contained characters who are never in trouble, never unhappy or ill, never make mistakes, and always count their change when it is handed to them.—Catherine Drinker Bowen

"Who are you looking at?"

Ever since the whole stamps thing started, I've been spending a ridiculous amount of time near the table in the front hall at school. Often, I rush to my locker between classes and don't talk to anybody just so I can make a quick trip past the table outside the office. I have no idea what I'm trying to accomplish by keeping an eye on the table—I mean, most of the time I'm in a classroom anyway so anybody could go to the table and leave a whole busload of Tamolinos boxes there and I'd never know.

The absolute last person I ever expected to see leaning over the table is Eric.

"Eric?"

"That's my name."

"Eric . . ."

"Heather . . ." We both start speaking at the same time and then stop.

"We have to talk," Eric says more seriously than I've ever heard him speak before.

He takes a step away from the table and I gasp.

"What's wrong with you?" he asks. "Can't someone make a donation?"

"Sure. Of course you can. It's just that . . . never mind. I didn't know you were into . . ." I catch myself before I say "Tamolinos underwear" and finish my sentence with "I didn't know you liked stamps."

"I don't. But we should still talk. At lunch. By the swings at the elementary school playground."

He doesn't leave any room for me to argue, which annoys me but I figure I probably need to talk to him as much as he seems to need to talk to me. I wonder if maybe he has information about the stolen stamps or something and somehow knows I'm friends with Alyssum. It's more than a little creepy how everyone on this island seems to know everyone else's business. He doesn't seem particularly mad or anything, so I decide I don't need to find someone to come along for protection. I've come to the conclusion that I was being a bit paranoid about the chemist-murderer stuff anyway.

"Fine."

He doesn't wait for me to say anything else. He snatches up his skateboard from where it leans against the wall and trots off down the hall.

In science class we're building models of volcanoes. For the second time in as many days I find myself up to my elbows in papier mâché goop, slithering strips of slimy newspaper over the outside of a chicken wire frame.

By lunch, I'm beside myself with curiosity about what Eric wants to talk about. Unfortunately, Steffie gets to me before I can grab my lunch out of my locker.

"Where are you going?" she asks. Her voice is sort

135

of sweet and kind, like someone in a bad movie who is talking to a very little kid, but you can tell they are just acting and really want to be on a cruise in the Caribbean.

"Lunch." I turn away from her but she moves around me so she's standing between me and my locker door.

"With us, right?"

Behind her, Su and Terri have appeared out of nowhere.

"Ah . . . actually I . . ."

"You know, it's lucky I'm not the kind of person to get hurt feelings because you are the kind of person who might hurt my feelings by ignoring me."

"I'm not ignoring you." It's not actually a complete lie. I'm not ignoring her, exactly. I'm hiding from her and avoiding her. That's not quite the same thing. "If I were ignoring you, I wouldn't be standing here talking to you, would I?"

"Where are you going for lunch?"

"Just outside. I have to go to the elementary school to meet . . . to meet my little brother, Matt."

I rack my brains to think whether or not I told the girls about my brother. I don't think I mentioned that he home-schools. I sure hope not, anyway.

"Your brother?"

"Yeah. I . . . I grabbed his lunch by mistake so we have to trade. I'll be back soon. Then I'll come and find you and we can sit together, okay?" Part of me wonders why on earth I'm trying so hard to stay friends with someone I don't even like and who, I'm beginning to suspect, doesn't particularly like me, either.

She seems satisfied with my answer, though, and nods. "Let's go, girlfriends . . . little Heather here will be back soon, won't she?"

"Sure." And, when I say it, I really don't think I'll be down at the elementary school playground for very long. After all, saying sorry doesn't take more than a couple of minutes and whatever Eric has to say can't possibly be that interesting.

Eric looks at his watch when I finally arrive.

"Sorry. I don't have wheels like some people."

He gives me a half grin and then looks very hard at the ground. I find a place to sit on the bottom of the slide opposite the teeter-totter where Eric has already taken his sandwich out of his lunch bag. Since officially Eric is the one who requested this meeting I figure he should be the first one to talk. He eats half his sandwich and I'm about ready to scream in frustration for him to get on with it when he finally says something. And what he says nearly knocks me over.

"I'm sorry."

"You're sorry? What on earth for? I'm the one who was a total jerk. I should never have said those things in front of your friends. I didn't mean them. I'm the one who's sorry. I had it all planned! How I was going to apologize to you, I mean."

We stare at each other for a moment and it's hard to tell which of us is more shocked.

"I'm sorry," I say again. "I shouldn't have interrupted you. Why are you apologizing?"

"For not being more sensitive."

This sounds so corny I burst out laughing. "What?!"

He holds up his hand like he's directing traffic. "I shouldn't have read those things out loud—I should have mailed them to you or something."

Ah-ha! He's not really apologizing at all. He only said sorry to trick me into saying sorry and spilling my guts.

Eric starts talking again and I'm glad he does because otherwise I might have said something I really would have regretted later.

"And, I know how hard it must be for you to start a new school and not have friends and stuff."

"I have friends," I interrupt.

He rolls his eyes. "The Steff-monster? Some friend. You know what she said about you?"

"What?"

"She's going around telling everyone they should build a psych ward at the hospital and name it after the Blake family."

I'm so stunned I can't think of a single thing to say. Eric drops his eyes to the ground and shakes his head a little from side to side, like he's trying to shake off a fly. "Steffie's mom works at the hospital," he mumbles. "She said both your mom and your grandmother have been in there with . . . with psychiatric problems."

He looks at me then and I guess he can see that my hands are shaking so hard my paper lunch bag is rustling. "I'm sorry," he says again.

Slowly, I stand up and turn away from him. The big soccer field shared by both schools is in front of me. Beyond that there's a stand of trees. My eyes fill up with tears and I start walking toward those trees. If I can just get there without bawling, I'll be okay, I think.

"Heather!"

Eric's voice sounds like it's coming from eight million miles away.

"Heather—you're not allowed to leave the school grounds!"

I don't care. I keep walking anyway. One step and then another and then another and then I'm running as fast as I can towards the trees on the far side of the field. I run until I can hardly breathe, run until my chest feels like it's about to tear right open, run until hot tears splash over my cheeks and I can hear horrible rasping sounds coming out of my mouth.

I keep on going until I get to the low fence at the end of the field. I climb over and stumble into the woods where I stop and sink onto my knees and bury my face in my hands and cry and cry and cry.

What does it matter if they expel me for leaving the school grounds? Who cares? At least if I get expelled I won't have to face anyone again. And then I start pounding my fists on the ground and tearing up clods of dirt and throwing them around because I am so mad I can't stand it any more! Who does Steffie think she is anyway, telling something like that to the whole school? What right does her mom have to talk about stuff that happens at work? And even stupider than Steffie is Mom who can't just get over Grandpa dying and Granny is ridiculous with her fake exploding heart and Eric is an idiot for telling me and then I can't believe I would think such horrible things and I throw another lump of dirt and another and another because I'm mad at Grandpa for dying and at me for making such a complete mess of everything. I hurl one final clod at a log and it explodes into the air like a globby bomb.

Then a strange thing happens. I take a deep, shuddering breath, sit up on my heels, still kneeling in the dirt, and I just feel completely empty and small and stupid.

"Are you okay? Should I get someone?"

Eric's voice is tentative. Worried. I feel like throwing up when I realize he must have seen my hysterical dirt-hurling fit. Maybe he thinks I'm crazy, too.

"I shouldn't have said anything. I'm sorry. I didn't say it to be mean. I just thought you should know what she was telling people. I'm . . ."

"It's okay." At this point, I figure Eric must already think I'm a total idiot so I don't even bother to put on any kind of brave act. I study the black lines of dirt under my nails and say, "Thank you for telling me. She's not really the kind of person I would normally make friends with."

"Oh?" he says. "What kind of person would you normally make friends with?"

"I like writers," I say with a sniffle.

"Yeah, we're the best," he nods.

That makes me smile despite the uneasy pitching in my stomach.

"We should go back," he says. "We really will get into trouble if they find us here. At least to the other side of the fence. We could stay there until you feel better."

And that's how I get to be sitting on the cold grass of the field with my back against the fence chatting with someone I thought was my mortal enemy.

"So, who is the stamp collector in your family if it's not you?" I ask, determined to keep the conversation away from my family. Besides, I'm not sure how long our truce will last so I figure I might as well try to get whatever information I can out of him.

"My grandfather."

"So he was the one who gave you the Tamolinos box?"

"Sort of. Granddad puts the stamps out on the kitchen counter. Mom's actually the one who boxes them up. I don't think she usually puts them in Tamolinos boxes. Sometimes she uses big brown envelopes or if there aren't many stamps, plastic sandwich bags. Anyway, Granddad goes through his new stamps and sorts them into those he wants to keep, those he wants to trade, and those that are so common he wants to get rid of them. The really common ones are the stamps he donates to your friend's project."

I nod. I doubt that Eric has any idea just how interested I am in finding out about his grandfather's stamp-collecting habits.

"The really valuable ones he puts in special albums or sometimes he makes these sort of display books with special stamp album pages in them for certain sub-collections."

"I know." It just slips out and I could just about bite my tongue off. For an instant I hope against hope that he didn't notice what I said.

"You know?" His eyes narrow. "How would you know that unless . . ."

"No! I didn't steal the stamps."

"How else would you know how Granddad organizes his stamps?"

There's no way around it. I have to tell him. "Because the Russian stamps, in their folder, showed up on the stamp table and Alyssum recognized them as being really valuable."

"So why didn't you tell me?"

"Why should I? I had no idea your grandfather was the owner of the stamps. I thought maybe your mother had stolen them," I confessed.

"My mother?" Now it was his turn to look horrified. "Why on earth would my mother steal Granddad's stamps? And if she had stolen them, why would she put them on the table? Why wouldn't she sell them or something?"

I shake my head. "I don't know. All I know is those stamps somehow got donated. Could it have been an accident?"

Eric looks thoughtful. "I don't think so. My grandfather is getting really old and he's got some problems with his memory," Eric admits. "Sometimes he gets confused and forgets where he puts stuff."

"Does he have Alzheimer's or something? Could he have donated the stamps by mistake? You know, put the wrong stamps out for your mom or something?" I've heard of Alzheimer's and how old people sometimes lose their memories completely.

Eric shakes his head. "No, it's not that bad. He's pretty organized as long as he sticks to his lists and keeps to his normal routine. That's why our family didn't report the stamps as being stolen at first. We thought Granddad had just misplaced them. But misplacing them in the house and putting them by the back door to take to the school are two completely different things. There's no way Granddad would have given away his valuable stamps."

"Are you sure?"

Eric looks a little exasperated, like he can't believe I would question him.

"Yes, I'm sure. I know my grandfather. He may be old but his stamp collection is his passion. There's no way he would make a mistake like that."

"So how on earth did the stamps get to the school?"

Eric shakes his head, completely baffled. Instead of

clearing things up, talking to Eric has just made things even more confusing.

"Maybe," he says, "they aren't the same stamps at all."

This hasn't occurred to me. I think it would be pretty tough for a thief to find matching Tamolinos boxes . . . and it's way too much of a coincidence that the missing stamps are from Russia just like the ones that showed up at Alyssum's.

"Maybe you should come over to Alyssum's," I say. "Would you recognize the stamps?"

"No," Eric says. "Granddad has thousands and thousands of stamps. They all look the same to me."

I can't hide my disappointment. "Oh, well, there's no point in coming to look then."

Eric winks at me and grins. "Sure there is," he says. "I may not know one stamp from another, but I would recognize my grandfather's handwriting from a mile away. He makes notes beside each stamp— about its value and condition and stuff. If I can look at the Russian stamps I could tell you if they come from my grandfather's collection."

"Then I guess you'd better come over," I say decisively. "Give me your phone number and I'll call you when I find out from Alyssum when it's okay for you to come over. Okay?"

"Okay. Sounds good. Call me tonight."

"Can I ask you one more thing before we go back?" Eric nods and stands up. "Why do you always hide under the table at the writing group?"

Eric turns a deep shade of red and laughs.

"It's dumb," he says. Then he blurts out, "Because I hate people looking at what I write. I freeze up if I think someone's watching me write."

"Really?" This is an astounding piece of information.

143

Mr. Supreme Self-confidence, Mr. Super-Mystery-Writer is so insecure he doesn't want anyone to watch him as he works?

"Yeah, well. I'd thank you not to mention it to anyone like, say, Wynd."

I laugh. "No problem."

We start walking back across the field together and I feel more relaxed than I have for weeks. In a weird way, I'm almost relieved someone knows about what's going on at home. I feel a bit better after my explosion, like a heavy rain cloud that's been punctured and spilled its contents.

Crossing the field in silence, my thoughts tumble over each other. Who would have known Eric had a self-conscious side? What kind of person would tell her daughter about patients at the hospital? And then, I start thinking about Maggie. I might be able to answer her letter after all.

Chapter Seventeen

"Heather?" Matt is outside Dove Cottage. "Heather, are you in there?"

He knows very well I'm in here. He saw me staggering across the driveway with a heavy box of books. I've decided to keep my favourites out here in case I need them for reference or inspiration. I make a mental note to retrieve *The Lion, the Witch, and the Wardrobe* from my backpack. It seems a bit silly to lug it back and forth to school every day. I haven't looked at it once on the school bus.

"Heather?"

Why is he bothering me? He knows I was upset when I grabbed the box and took off when Mom and Granny arrived home. I had hoped they would walk in and Mom would smile and be back to normal, but it didn't happen that way at all. Mom barely looked at Matt or me and it was Granny who gave us each a hug.

Mia raced around Mom's feet in little delighted circles but instead of bending over and giving her a big hug, Mom just looked sort of irritated with the dog and said, "We're home," in the same funny, flat voice I remembered from when she phoned from Ontario. "Kids, give your dad a hand with dinner. Momma—put your feet up and take it easy."

"But dear, I'm perfectly fine."

Matt ran over to Mom and wrapped his arms around her waist and she patted him weakly on the head and said, "Hi, Mattie. I'm tired." She looked at Granny and said, "I don't feel like arguing just now. I think I'd better lie down for a little while. Later on I have to spend some time in my office. I'm getting so far behind. . . ."

A thousand nasty things came to my mind, like doesn't she know how mean she's being? I could feel all these accusations welling up inside me and before I could say anything I turned and stalked out of the house and came out here to escape from everyone.

"Heather? Can I come in?"

Mattie sounds like he's about five years old and not nine and three-quarters.

"Come in. What do you want?"

Matt doesn't say anything. He stands in the doorway and when I look at him properly I realize his cheeks are streaked with tears and his nose is running.

"Hey, Mattie—what's up?"

"Who's going to die next? Mom or Granny?"

"What are you talking about?"

Matt is really crying hard now, his slim shoulders hopping up and down with every sob. "Why . . . why . . . why don't they just tell us? What's wrong with Mom? Why does she have to sleep all the time? And what about Granny?"

I really don't know what to say. Now there's another reason to be mad at Dad. I knew he should have told Matt what was going on, right from the beginning.

"Nobody is dying," I say firmly.

"Why is Mom still so tired? And Granny's heart . . ." Matt dissolves into another round of crying.

"Matt . . . hey, come on. If Granny were really sick she'd still be in the hospital, right?"

I reach out to touch his shoulder and he pulls away.

"What did Dad tell you?" I ask.

"Just that Granny had a lot of stress and that can make you feel worried and make your heart beat funny. But that's how you get heart attacks, isn't it?"

Dad did a lousy job of explaining. "Did he mention panic attacks?" Matt looks blank. I try to explain how Granny had suffered a big shock, like all of us, when Grandpa died, and how she just kept going and going and how it all just overwhelmed her and she sort of panicked. It wasn't very technical but it was the best I could come up with.

"So her heart is okay?"

I nod.

"For sure?"

"For sure."

His bottom lip starts to tremble again. "But what about Mom? She's not panicking. She has something serious. Or why else would she be so tired and not working?"

"Look, if she was really desperately sick, she'd be in the hospital, right?"

"Not necessarily. Maybe they want her to have her last weeks here with us. . . . Granny knows all about it and that's the real reason why she panicked." At this thought his crying gets louder. I suck my bottom lip between my teeth and search desperately for something to say that will make him feel better.

Why didn't Dad talk to him? Why am I the one who has to do all the explaining when I don't even really understand what's going on?

"Do you want to go down to the rope swing?"

147

Matt blinks at me through his tears like this is the stupidest idea I've ever come up with. The rope swing is beside the stream that cuts through the bottom part of our farm. The stream runs through a small forest of huge old cedars and Douglas fir trees. Some of the trees have pale green moss hanging from their branches, just like they're from a Hollywood movie set. I haven't been down to the stream since school started.

"I'll tell you everything I know," I promise. "And we can see if the swinging rope is still there."

He nods and snuffles his nose into the sleeve of his thick sweater.

The shadows are already long when we get to the edge of the forest. When we discovered the place in the summer, we made up a silly game. We pretended that the trees had spirits and we needed to ask permission to enter their world.

"Oh, mighty cedars, let us pass," Matt says seriously.

"May the tree spirits protect us. . . ." I reply.

We turn in place three times and then hold our arms out for balance as we step carefully along the trunk of a fallen tree. If either of us slips and falls, we both have to go back to the edge of the forest and start all over again.

At the far end of the log we can just make out the gurgle of the stream meandering through the trees. Matt jumps off the end of the log, touches his fingertips to the red bark of the great cedar that stands sentry beside the stream, and then bounces lightly from one boulder to the next across the stepping stone bridge we built during the summer. On the far side, we both stroke our hands along the exposed roots of a Douglas fir tree and then climb up the small embankment, using the roots as steps.

The swing is at the top of the bank, a heavy length

of rope knotted at the bottom. It hangs motionless in the shadows, waiting silently for our return.

"Me first," Matt says. He reaches up as high as he can on the rope and hoists himself up until he is standing on the knot. I grab hold of the end of the rope and run past him, lifting his feet and then letting go so he swings back over the creek, shrieking and laughing as he flies backwards through the air.

When, after a few minutes, he jumps off beside me, he catches the rope and offers it to me. Earlier in the summer I would have taken the rope and jumped on, enjoying the swoosh of the wind through my hair as I swung out and back, out and back.

But now, looking at Matt's tear-streaked face, I feel like jumping on a rope swing isn't important, that it's too babyish. Though I take the rope from him, I don't scramble up onto the knot. Instead, I stand in front of him and say, "Mom has something called depression."

He looks at me blankly.

"That means she has a kind of deep sadness that won't go away." I try to remember what Dad told me and how the library book described it.

"You mean, because of Grandpa?"

I nod. "Kind of. I mean, that's what started it. But sometimes people don't get better right away from being sad. Sometimes it takes a while and sometimes they have to take pills to help them get better."

Matt looks at me, his eyes glistening in the gathering darkness under the trees. "So Mom doesn't have cancer? She's not going to die?"

I shake my head firmly. "Nope."

"So, when will she get better?"

I was hoping Matt wouldn't ask about that. Nobody seems to know. "Well, she is taking some special pills and hopefully soon they will start working." I hope this is enough to satisfy Matt.

"That's all she has to do? Take pills?"

"Actually, I think she's going to see a counsellor, too. Dad says sometimes it helps to talk about things."

"Are you going to swing, or what?"

Matt finally seems satisfied that neither Mom nor Granny is about to die and he can't understand why I'm not jumping on the rope.

"Go ahead—you can have another turn."

He looks at me like I'm crazy—in the summer we were always fighting about having longer turns swinging off the bank. That doesn't stop him from taking the rope back and climbing aboard. I give him a good, hard push and he swings way out over the creek in a sweeping arc.

"Yeeeee-haaaah!" he yells, and the trees ring with his laughter.

"You are not going anywhere," Dad says firmly.

"Why not?"

"I want you to stick around and help out with dinner. And don't roll your eyes like that—they'll get stuck in the back of your head!"

I stare helplessly at the phone. I know Eric is waiting for me to call but I can't talk to him until I've spoken with Alyssum to see if it's okay to go over to her house. There's no point in arguing. I'm hardly surprised to hear Mom is back in her room. Hiding, it seems to me. When Granny suggests that we take her a bowl of soup I feel like saying that we shouldn't waste good food on someone who isn't going to eat it anyway.

Matt asks if he can take in the soup and I just hope that he doesn't say anything to Mom about our conversation by the creek. As he walks slowly down the hallway with a bowl of mulligatawny soup balanced on a tray, I feel another twinge of irritation, this time about how annoying it is that I'm caught in the middle of having to tell Matt half-truths because none of the grown-ups seem to want to talk to him like he's a real person.

Mom doesn't come out for dinner, but when Granny goes to retrieve the tray from Mom's room, she shows it to us silently when she comes back to the kitchen. The soup bowl is nearly empty and half the dinner roll is gone. Mom has even eaten a bit of the salad and a little rice, too.

It's totally ridiculous, but when I see the effort Mom has made to eat, I feel a burst of pride and relief, like this is the biggest accomplishment anyone could make. When Granny cuts a slice of pie for Mom, I volunteer to take it down the hall to give it to her. When I let myself into the bedroom, Mom is sitting up and she actually looks at me and says "thank you" when I hand her the plate of dessert.

"Wow," she says softly. "I don't think I can manage such a big piece. I'll give it a try though—it sure looks good."

I smile at her and put the tray on the bed. That's the most she's said to me for ages and I can't believe how good it makes me feel to see her sitting up.

"Can I get you anything else?" I ask.

"I think this is fine," she says, and I feel another little thrill that she's still talking instead of nodding or, worse, staring at the wall like I don't exist. "Actually," she says when my hand is on the doorknob, "would you mind making me a cup of tea? That would be lovely."

"Sure!" I let myself out into the hall and fly down to the kitchen. I plug in the kettle and as I rinse out the teapot and root around in the cupboards for Mom's favourite kind of tea, I'm surprised to find that I'm humming to myself.

Granny comes into the kitchen from her dining room bedroom as I'm unplugging the kettle. She carefully puts a small blue ceramic vase on the table.

"Milly brought this for us," she says. "That was thoughtful, don't you think?"

"Mom asked for a cup of tea," I interrupt.

Granny smiles and brushes my bangs out of my eyes. She nods and says, "I think your mom's starting to feel a little better."

A feeling of sympathy wells up inside me. The past weeks must have been awful for Granny. She has tried so hard to stay calm, optimistic, to look after all of us. She has never once complained, not about losing Grandpa, or about Mom, not even about her makeshift bedroom right beside the kitchen. *Stoic.* That's a good word to describe her.

Inside, though, she must be anything but serene. Maybe being stoic is dangerous. Maybe she should talk about how she's feeling. Maybe that way she wouldn't hide her sadness inside so it bursts out of her in a panic.

"Would you like a cup of tea?" I ask.

Writer Girl looks into the eyes of the older woman, longing to tell her she understands something about hiding unhappiness. She wants to share secrets—she wants to know the old woman's trick for remaining so calm even when her world is falling apart around her. In exchange, she would think of something wise and profound to say about sharing. Writer Girl says nothing. She has no such piece of wisdom to offer. The lines at the corners of the grandmother's eyes deepen as she smiles.

152

"Thank you, Heather. Tea would be lovely. Earl Grey?"

"Sure. Granny, are you lonely?"

"Lonely? Of course I miss your grandfather terribly." Her voice catches in her throat. "But it's easier being here than at home on the farm where everything I looked at or touched reminded me of him. It's not good to live in the past, Heather. It's lovely to be here with all of you."

"Maybe you could make friends with Milly," I suggest. "You know, someone to talk to."

Granny wraps her hands around her empty teacup as if to warm it up. "You're probably right. I've been feeling like I have to help everybody else since I got here—but you know, everyone needs a friend to talk to. You are absolutely right about that."

I watch her carefully, fascinated by the changing play of emotions over her face as she seems to will herself to look at the bright side in her situation.

Everyone needs someone to talk to, I think bitterly, including Matt. "I told Matt about everything."

The smile fades from Granny's eyes and she leans forward and rests her elbows on the kitchen table.

"We all wanted to protect him," Granny says finally. She no longer looks brave and stoic. She looks weary. Defeated. "We thought he was too young to understand about your mother. And how do you explain a panic attack to such a little boy?" She traces her fingertip over the edge of a rose thorn on the tablecloth pattern and looks vaguely embarrassed.

"He's not so little, you know. He sees a lot. He under-stands a lot." I set a cup of tea in front of her. "It's better to know the truth," I say, feeling a little defensive.

Granny nods. "I'm sorry, Heather. Your dad and I should have talked to him. Poor Matt. Poor you—it wasn't your job to say anything."

"Matt's okay," I say. "He's smarter than you think."

She nods again and sips her tea. She seems at a loss for words. Panic attacks or not, I don't want to make it easy for her. I was the one who saw Matt weeping his heart out because he thought everyone was dying. Granny is one of the grown-ups. She should have known better.

"Why don't you take that tea to your mother?" Granny says.

"Where is Dad?" I ask when I get back a few minutes later.

"In his studio. He's determined to finish the two paintings." She sets her cup on the table like she's come to a decision. "Why don't we go and pay him a little visit? The three of us should really talk."

"What about Matt?" I suppress my exasperation. Wasn't she listening to me?

"Of course. You are absolutely right, Heather. Let's all go to the studio and have a word with your father."

"In his studio?" Surely Granny knows Dad doesn't like people dropping by to visit. Nobody is allowed to go into his studio unless the house is burning down.

"This is important, Heather. Your father will understand. And so will your mother—I'll go and get her. She should be in on this discussion, too."

Chapter Eighteen

The phone is ringing as I walk back into the house
after our family conference in Dad's studio. Usually I
hate family meetings but this time it was a big relief
to admit to each other how worried we've all been. I
feel much better now that we've all sat down and
talked about Mom and Granny and what we might
expect over the next few weeks.

Dad and Granny did most of the talking and they
did a much better job of explaining everything than
I had. And I learned something, too. Granny and Dad
are also going to see a counsellor and Mom and
Granny are joining a meditation group together.
They even offered us the option of coming to a family
counselling session if we wanted to.

Matt wasn't babyish at all, which didn't surprise
me in the least.

The jangling phone forces me to stop replaying bits
of the conversation in my head. I snatch the receiver
out of its cradle mid-ring. "Hello?"

"Hi, Heather? It's Eric."

"Oh, hi! Can I call you right back? I didn't get a
chance to call Alyssum."

"Sure."

I hang up and dial the Cranwells' number. The phone rings and rings and finally the answering machine picks up. I leave a message and then call Eric back.

"They're not home!"

"Oh." The disappointment in his voice is obvious.

I try to think of something else to say, something to take his mind off not being able to come over to look at the stamps. "How is your writing group assignment coming along?"

This week we have to describe an airport using all of our senses.

"Oh, fine I guess. I've been a little distracted." I can sure understand what he means. It's hard to write when there's so much going on. "I'm trying to write the scene from the point of view of a criminal, to see if someone like that notices different things."

"It would sure be easier to do that if you knew a real criminal," I say, trying to make conversation.

"Well, I do know a criminal. But it doesn't help."

"You do?" I hope I don't sound too shocked. "I've never met a real-life criminal."

"Oh yes you have," he says.

"I have? Who?"

"Wynd."

"What? Wynd from the writing group?"

"Yup. She's been arrested for shoplifting and then she got into all that trouble with the cigarette sales."

"Cigarette sales?"

"Don't you read the paper?"

"Not all the time. . . ." I say a little defensively.

"Well, check out the paper from two or three weeks ago. There's a story in there about her latest escapade. You do recycle, don't you?"

"Yes. I'll look and see if it's still around somewhere."

"I've gotta go. Will you call me later?"

"If I can get hold of Alyssum. Otherwise I guess I'll just be working in Dove Cottage on our assignment."

"Dove Cottage? What's that?"

"It's my writing cottage. Dad and I renovated one of our outbuildings so now I have somewhere private to write."

"You're lucky. I wish I had somewhere like that to work. I have a desk in my room, but a real writer's cottage would be way better."

I nod at my end of the phone and say, "Yeah. It's great—a little cold, but it is pretty inspiring to have a quiet place to go." Not many people understand why I prefer to shiver in a renovated chicken coop rather than write at a comfortable desk in my room. Somehow I know I don't have to explain to Eric.

We hang up and I head for the recycling box. Unfortunately, it's nearly empty.

"Where are all the newspapers?"

"Check the little guys' room," Dad answers.

Inwardly, I groan. We use newspapers to line the bottoms of the cages. I hope the guinea pig hasn't chewed up the paper I'm looking for. There's a big stack of papers by the door of the little guys' room, but the paper I'm looking for isn't there. It's impossible to tell the date of the papers in the rodents' cages—the rats and the guinea pig are pretty efficient chewers. I've resigned myself to having to phone Eric back and ask him to read the article to me when I have a peek in the bottom of Snow's cage.

As usual, the budgie has made a terrible mess of her cage. Bits of food and seed husks are spattered all over the place and the paper underneath her bath is soggy from where she splashed water everywhere. For a little bird, she certainly leaves lots of droppings in just one day. Of course, the date on the top of the paper is the one I'm looking for. Carefully I fish out several layers of newspaper and shake off the loose stuff into the garbage. Snow peeps and whistles as she scuttles from one end of her perch to the other.

"Here. I'll give you some more paper."

I replace the paper with fresh from the pile and then spread my find out on the floor. It only takes a minute to find the article.

Local Teen Responsible for Store Fine

The headline is over an article about a girl working in the Singing Pelican corner store and how she was caught selling cigarettes to her friends. Though it doesn't say her name because she is underage, I know the article is talking about Wynd.

Since it's illegal to sell cigarettes to anyone under the age of nineteen the store was fined a thousand dollars and has been forbidden to sell cigarettes to anyone (of legal age or not) for six months. The article goes on to say that the girl will not lose her job but will be expected to pay the fine.

A thousand dollars. Wow. Wynd can't be getting paid very much to work at the store and if that's her only source of income it's going to take her a very long time to pay the money back. I wonder what will happen to her if she doesn't pay? I wonder if she will go to some sort of jail for juvenile delinquents?

A light bulb pops on in Writer Girl's head. So that's what Steffie meant when she said her source for cigarettes was unreliable.

The most interesting part about the next writing group meeting is not what people read (it turns out airports are pretty easy places to write about), but the argument Eric has with Willow about halfway through the evening.

"She's probably in jail," Eric jokes when Gillian asks if he knows why Wynd isn't at the meeting. "Or grounded."

"You shouldn't talk about people who aren't here," Willow says.

"You shouldn't be so sensitive," Eric snaps back. "Besides, it's not gossip when the information is factual."

"So, you're saying it's a fact Wynd is in jail?"

"No. That was a joke. But I'm serious that she is probably grounded. She and her dad had a huge fight at our house."

"At your house?" This seems bizarre. Why would Wynd and her father be at Eric's house?

"Her dad is our housekeeper. Wynd sometimes meets him there so she can get a ride home."

"Your housekeeper?"

Eric can't hide his irritation at being interrupted.

"Mr. Bell cleans half the houses on this island," Willow says. "What were they fighting about?"

"Mr. Bell?" I'm about six steps behind this conversation but I'm determined to catch up. "Not the same Mr. Bell from our school?"

Eric glares at me. "Mr. Bell—our secretary. Yes. He cleans houses part-time and works at the school part-time. His wife left him after Mr. Bell had an affair with the post-mistress."

I'm horrified at the idea. Gloria at the post office must be near retirement age. "He had an affair with Gloria?!"

Willow laughs. "No, of course not. This all happened a few years ago when Sabine Rotenburg was in charge of the post office. She left the island because the gossip was too much for her."

159

"So, she's not part of Mr. Bell's life any more?" I ask, trying to keep the relationships straight.

"Not unless he's commuting to Winnipeg," Eric says. "That's where Sabine moved."

"Where's Wynd's mother?"

"Vancouver, I think," Willow answers. "Wynd goes there sometimes to visit."

"Why did Wynd decide to stay with her dad?"

Eric sighs with exasperation. "How should I know? I didn't even live here when all this was going on. Why don't you ask her?"

I shut my mouth. Apparently, the gossip only covers so much territory.

"You didn't answer my question, Eric," Willow interrupts. "Why were they fighting?"

"They were arguing about the money, of course."

"The cigarette fine?"

Eric nods. "Wynd wanted to buy some CDs with part of her paycheque and her dad said she had to use everything she earns at the store to pay off the fine. Then Wynd got really mad and told her dad he was selfish because he had changed his mind about helping her."

Eric looks like he is thoroughly enjoying relating this piece of scandal.

"What's that supposed to mean?"

Eric shrugs. "That's all I know. They left in a big huff. They were still yelling at each other when they got in their car and drove away."

We sit in an awkward silence for a minute before Eric says, "Well, we're done early tonight. Who wants to use the phone in the kitchen to call for rides?"

Willow, Gillian, and I all start to move towards the door at the back of the meeting room but I stop when I notice Eric making a 'wait here' gesture to me. The minute the other two girls have disappeared he whispers to me, "Wynd must have done it. She must have stolen the stamps to pay off the fine."

Of course! "What are we going to do about it?"

"I guess we'd better talk to her dad."

"We?"

"He's at the school tomorrow. We can talk to Mr. Bell then. He should know we're on to Wynd so she doesn't try to steal any more of Granddad's stamps." Eric's eyes flash with anger. "How could she steal from an old man?"

I shake my head. I have no answer. I can't believe anyone would have the nerve to steal in the first place, never mind joke around with the victim's grandson every week. It seems I have a lot to learn about the workings of the criminal mind.

Chapter Nineteen

Collected Quote #121
All writers are vain, selfish, and lazy, and at the very bottom of their motives there lies a mystery.—George Orwell

I'm glad Eric is beside me when we go into the office toward the end of the lunch hour. Mr. Bell is busy answering the phone, passing messages on to teachers, and calling a sick girl's mother to come and pick her up. We wait patiently in the two chairs until the bell rings to signal the end of the lunch hour.

There is a swell of noise from the halls as students crash in and out of their lockers and swarm to their next classes. There aren't that many students at the high school, but when they're all in the halls at the same time it sounds like there are ten thousand kids milling around.

"Won't you two be late?" Mr. Bell asks.

"We have to talk to you about something," Eric says.

"Right now?"

"It's about Wynd."

Mr. Bell takes off his glasses and rubs his eyes like he's suddenly very weary. "What has she done now?" he asks.

Eric clears his throat. "You remember those stamps that went missing? There was an article in the paper about it."

Mr. Bell nods uneasily and Eric continues. "We think Wynd stole them. She comes to our house with you sometimes and you know Granddad collects stamps and so does she. She could easily have seen the stamps and taken them, thinking maybe she could sell them to raise enough money to pay her fine."

Mr. Bell's eyes are watery and grey. He sighs heavily and shakes his head. "Not Wynd. It wasn't her."

"Who else could it have been? She's the only person I can think of who has a motive and access to our house. I wanted to tell you before I tell my mom. She'll want to report it to the police."

That had been my idea, to report everything to the police. Eric, though, wanted to give Mr. Bell a chance to prepare himself so he wouldn't go into shock when the police arrived at his door to arrest Wynd.

Mr. Bell shakes his head again. "No," he says deliberately. "Wynd did not steal the stamps."

I totally understand why he would want to protect his daughter. She's in enough trouble as it is.

"But—"

Mr. Bell puts up his hand to silence Eric. "No, Eric. I know for certain my daughter is innocent of that particular crime. I am the one who stole the stamps."

I nearly fall over with shock. "What?!" I'm way out of my depth here. The last thing on earth I expected was for Mr. Bell to lie and pretend he had committed the crime. It is amazing how far some people will go to protect their children.

He nods and continues. "Eric, you'd better call your mother. And the police, I guess. There's no point in hiding the truth any longer."

Eric's mother and a young constable arrive at the

school a short time later followed by Alyssum, her mother, and the stamps. It was my idea to call the Cranwells, just in case we weren't even talking about the same stamps, though that seemed less and less likely with every passing minute. Eric and I haven't moved from our seats in the office. We figure we're already going to be in trouble for cutting classes so we may as well stick around to see what happens.

The school office is pretty crowded and when the principal, Mrs. Gurney, sees who is gathering, she suggests we all move into her office. It's no bigger than the waiting area but at least it's private. Though, let's face it, nothing stays private on this island.

Once we are all gathered inside, Mr. Bell shifts in his chair but doesn't say anything.

Alyssum clears her throat and says, "We brought the stamps." We all turn to look at her. I can't believe she would speak in front of a room full of people and a police officer.

Mrs. Cranwell looks shocked when she sees the Tamolinos box, still dusty with fingerprint powder. "So that's why you wanted . . ."

She's interrupted by Eric's mother who lifts the lid of the box and exclaims, "The Russian stamps!"

"So those are the stolen stamps?" the constable says.

She nods mutely and we all look back at Mr. Bell.

"I'm so terribly sorry," he begins, and from the way he's holding his jaw so stiffly it looks like he's fighting not to start crying. I've never felt more uncomfortable in my whole life.

"Ahhh . . . you've all heard about the trouble over the cigarettes?" Everyone nods. "It has been so hard for us since Angela . . . since all the trouble." He looks decidedly pained. It must be awful to know that all the details of your private life are common knowledge. He clears his throat uncomfortably and continues. "I thought . . . well, Wynd couldn't afford to lose her job and it seemed like if I could help her pay the fine quickly the whole mess could be forgotten but of course I don't have a thousand dollars lying around . . . and, Wynd hasn't been happy. She keeps threatening to leave and live with her mother and . . ."

"So you stole the stamps?" Eric asks. His mother looks horrified.

"I . . . wanted to help Wynd. She's not a bad girl—not at all. But she's had some hard times—it's been good for her to learn responsibility by having a job. The worst thing would have been for her to lose her job . . . I wanted her to stay here with me. I thought if I gave her the money she wouldn't run off to Vancouver."

Mr. Bell seems bewildered. Like I feel.

"But if you were going to sell the stamps, why did you put them on the donation table?" I don't plan to blurt out my question. It catches me by surprise. I cannot understand why, after stealing the stamps, Mr. Bell would have given them away again.

He nods. "I was going to take the stamps to Victoria and sell them. I called a stamp shop to see what they were worth and I nearly died when I found out how valuable they were. I wanted to put the stamps back, but I was terrified of getting caught. They'd been discovered missing and I knew Mrs. Maloney had turned the house upside down looking for them. I couldn't think how to return them—where to put them. . . . I just didn't know what to do so I went for a walk at Grey's Point. . . ."

"Grey's Point?" The constable is making notes as Mr. Bell talks.

"I always walk the length of the beach and back whenever I have to think things through. Anyway, I went for a long walk and by the time I got back I realized it wouldn't help Wynd at all to just give her the money. Part of learning to take responsibility for her actions is learning to accept the consequences."

"But you had already stolen the stamps. . . ." Eric's mother says softly.

Mr. Bell nods unhappily. "I tell you, I didn't know what to do. I couldn't admit to having stolen them or half my income would have disappeared. Who would want to hire a housekeeper who is also a thief? I didn't want to destroy them—they're fascinating stamps. So I thought if I donated them, at least the money would go to a good cause. That was the best idea I could come up with."

He puts his face in his hands and shakes his head sadly from side to side. "I'm so sorry," he moans.

"Mrs. Maloney?"

Eric's mother looks at the police officer.

"Would you like to press charges?"

The tension in the room is unbearable as Mrs. Maloney looks first at the top of Mr. Bell's balding head, then at Eric, and then back at the constable.

"I'll have to think about that," she says quietly. "Perhaps. But then again, I'm not sure what good would come of sending Mr. Bell to jail. We have the stamps back. There may be some other way for Mr. Bell to pay for his crime. I'll call you, Mr. Bell." She looks at the police officer again. "I'll let you know what I decide to do."

With that, she picks up the Tamolinos box, slips it under her arm, and graciously leaves the room. As the door closes behind her I realize that living on a small island where everyone knows everyone has certain advantages. In a big city, I suspect Mr. Bell would already be in handcuffs and on his way to jail. Here, though, it seems like nobody is particularly shocked that Mrs. Maloney didn't press charges right away, not even the police officer.

Those of us remaining in the office seem like we have been turned to stone. Nobody moves until the police officer says, "Well, I suppose you are free to go."

We all file out of the office. Everyone, that is, except Mr. Bell. He stays behind, sitting at Mrs. Gurney's desk looking totally stunned.

Chapter Twenty

Collected Quote #5
How can you write if you can't cry?—Ring Lardner

A week later, Alyssum, Matt, and I are covered in paint. With the help of some strategically placed bamboo support sticks, the salt and pepper shakers actually look like salt and pepper shakers. Alyssum stands back to admire the finished costumes. "They turned out really great, didn't they?"

I nod. "Fantastic."

"Will the paint be dry for tonight?" Matt asks.

"Sure. This doesn't take long to dry. We'll hang our UNICEF boxes around our 'lids' on strings. What about your costume, Heather? Is it all finished?"

I nod and smile. At first, Eric thought we should dress up in old-fashioned costumes and go to the school dance as Shakespeare and his wife. I told him that was a dumb idea since I was as good a writer as anyone and had no intention of going anywhere as Shakespeare's sidekick.

Being a famous writer was a good idea, though. So, I'm dressing up in a long dress and a bonnet and going as Jane Austen. First, Eric and I will take Matt and Alyssum to the Community Centre. The Seniors Society is holding the Kid-Fest and the firefighters have organized the big bonfire in the field behind the greenhouse. Then, after the younger kids get picked up, Eric and I are walking to the dance at the high school.

Eric made it very clear that he doesn't consider this a date or anything. "We're just two writers sticking together, okay?" is what he said. Which is fine with me.

December 1st
Dove Cottage, Tarragon Island
Hi, Maggie.

I can't believe I haven't written for so long. November just seemed to fly by. Since the Halloween dance I have hardly had time to think, never mind write letters. I thought you might like an update, though.

I think I told you in my last letter about going to the dance with Eric. We had a ton of fun—he was hilarious. He snuck his skateboard into the gym. I doubt William Shakespeare could even have imagined a crazier way to zoom around the dance floor!

I hardly ever talk to Steffie and Co. any more. I don't know if they are ignoring me or I'm ignoring them—whatever, the feeling is mutual. Remember I told you about Emma Patten and her friend Briony? We've started hanging out and I'm getting to know some of their friends, too.

Mr. Bell, you remember I told you about how he stole those stamps? Well, he has agreed to spend five hours every week helping Mr. Maloney, Senior with his stamp collection. That old man has millions of stamps. He was so happy to see his Russian stamps again that he gave Alyssum a reward of $100! She was pretty happy about that.

Wynd, the girl who caused all the trouble in the first place, didn't lose her job. She won't talk about anything that happened, but at the writing group she read this really interesting story about a girl who realizes her father is willing to go to jail for her. The girl decides to pay off her fine and not cause any more problems for her dad.

That's in her story, at least. Some days she still looks as grouchy as ever, and personally, I wonder how long she'll be able to stay out of trouble, or stay on the island, for that matter.

My mystery novel is going along great. I've decided to make it a triple murder. Eric is really helpful when it comes to figuring out how long it takes for a victim to die from stab wounds and stuff (it depends a lot on what part of the body gets stabbed), and now that I'm used to everyone, I can't wait to go to the writing group every week. Besides the writing we do, I am learning so much about the people who live on this island! If I just wrote down all the stories I hear I would have fifty novels worth of material already!

I put down my pen and stare at the wall for a minute. Once, I might have thought that Maggie would get jealous if she knew I was enjoying my new writing group, but I don't think that any more. She's a true friend and I know she will be happy for me. I know that if I could figure out a way to explain about my mother and about Granny, she would understand about all that, too.

Granny's been doing great. She's only had one more panic attack. She managed to get through it with deep breathing and relaxation techniques she's been learning at her meditation group. But explaining all that and what's been going on with Mom seems like it's way too complicated and I hardly know where to begin.

This morning at the breakfast table, the strangest thing happened. In our family we have a tradition that starts on the first day of December. Each year, my mother buys one of those Advent calendars with little pieces of chocolate hidden behind every door. Matt and I have to take turns opening a door every day between December first and Christmas.

Mom has slowly been getting better ever since she started taking those pills. She's been eating more, usually joins us at the table for meals, and doesn't need so many naps, but she's still not exactly her old self. Just to make sure we had one this year, I used some of my allowance to buy one of those calendars.

At the breakfast table today, I said, "I have a surprise!" and pulled out a chocolate-filled Advent calendar from under the table and showed it to everyone.

Matt squawked and said, "No way!" Then he ran out in the hall and came back a minute later with an Advent calendar he had bought.

We all started smiling and Matt and I were saying how it was great there were two calendars this year so we wouldn't have to share the chocolates when Dad said, "Guess what?" Of course, he had bought a calendar, too, and not only that, so had Granny!

When Granny pulled her Advent calendar out from the coat closet, we all started laughing, Mom the loudest. She laughed until she had to wipe her eyes with a corner of the tablecloth and then she said, "Honestly! You people have no faith in your mother! Do you really think I would forget the Advent calendar?"

And she went to the bedroom and brought back a fifth calendar! Once we had stopped laughing, we all counted to three and then we each found the door marked *1*, opened it, and had our own personal piece of chocolate.

The funniest thing was, when Dad and Matt left

the room to go and feed the cows, and Granny had her back to us at the sink, Mom and I smiled at each other so hard we both almost started crying. That's how it is, sometimes when I'm so relieved or so happy I can hardly stand it—I just want to cry.

I didn't, though. I got up and hugged my mom really, really hard. And she hugged me really, really hard right back.

Writer Girl stares at the piece of lavender writing paper on her desk. Part of her wants to tell her best friend about all the happiest places and all the saddest places in her soul. Instead, she signs her name at the bottom of the page, folds the letter in half, and slips it into the envelope. Sometimes, she thinks, there's no way to put the most important stuff in a letter. But it's not always necessary, either, because best friends are very good at reading between the lines.

I lick the back of the envelope and write a little message to Maggie on the back.

Greetings from your correspondent on Tarragon Island!

Then I blow out the candles and head back up to the house.

About the Author

Nikki Tate is a writer and professional storyteller who is popular at library and school readings. She lives with her daughter Danielle on the Saanich Peninsula of British Columbia's beautiful Vancouver Island. Tate has chosen to set her novels for children in her familiar countryside and the nearby Gulf Islands. "My lovely garden and the glorious views of Mount Baker and the Gulf Islands are my biggest enemies! How am I supposed to get any work done when I live in such spectacular surroundings?"

Also by Nikki Tate . . . the Bestselling StableMates Series!

StableMates 1: Rebel of Dark Creek—Meet Jessa, a grade six girl from Vancouver Island, who falls in love with a pony named Rebel. Jessa must learn to juggle school, barn chores, and friendship in this story of determination and ingenuity.

StableMates 2: Team Trouble at Dark Creek—Two giant draft horses arrive at Dark Creek Stables, and Jessa's pony, Rebel, finds himself out in the cold during the worst blizzard of the century. To complicate matters, Jessa and her best friend, Cheryl, have an argument, and an unexpected visitor almost ruins Jessa's Christmas vacation.

StableMates 3: Jessa Be Nimble, Rebel Be Quick—As an eventing clinic draws closer, Jessa needs to find a way to conquer her fears about water jumps. At school she's assigned to help Midori, a new student from Japan, settle in. Cheryl is no help at all—she's too busy trying to land a juicy part in a play.

StableMates 4: Sienna's Rescue—When four abused and neglected horses are seized by the Kenwood Animal Rescue Society, Jessa convinces Mrs. Bailey that Dark Creek Stables would be a perfect foster farm for one of them, but nobody is prepared for the challenges of Sienna's rehabilitation. Can Jessa and her friends save the young renegade mare from the slaughterhouse?

StableMates 5: Raven's Revenge—When Jessa wins a trip for two to horse camp, she and Cheryl are so excited they can hardly think of anything else. But Camp Singing Waters may not be a blissful getaway. Feuding campers, a lame horse and drafty cabins are bad enough, but should they have listened more carefully to Mrs. Bailey's ominous warning about Dr. Rainey's experiments with witchcraft? Or, are the late-night ghost stories around the campfire just fuelling their overactive imaginations?

StableMates 6: Return to Skoki Lake—Jessa's week-long trail riding trip into the Rocky Mountains should have been the experience of a lifetime. Ignoring increasingly peculiar symptoms, Jessa sets off into the mountains, determined to enjoy herself despite feeling very ill. To her horror, she finds herself regaining consciousness in an Alberta hospital bed! This is only the beginning of a long journey of recovery, one which turns Jessa's life upside down and threatens even her desire to ride.